ACCORDING TO
ROBIN

BY THE SAME AUTHOR

ACCORDING TO ROBIN

Julian Fane

Book Guild Publishing
Sussex, England

First published in Great Britain in 2006 by
The Book Guild Ltd
25 High Street
Lewes, East Sussex
BN7 2LU

Typesetting in Garamond by
Keyboard Services, Luton, Bedfordshire

Printed in Great Britain by
Antony Rowe Ltd, Chippenham, Wiltshire

A catalogue record for this book is available from
The British Library

ISBN 1 85776 979 1

Contents

1

Sunday evening in a northern suburb of London in the twenty-first century, the month November and the time seven o'clock.

It was dark and it was drizzling. The scene was Roebuck Road. Terrace houses faced each other across the road, one end of which was dominated by the blocks of flats known as Roebuck Buildings; at the other end Coronation Street wound into Village Way and on to Boroughfare that linked with the M1.

Four streetlamps cast yellowish light on the two lines of parked cars. Several cars were wrecks awaiting collection by the Highway Department of the Council: their wheels had been pinched and their windows bashed in. There were a couple of self-assembly roofless two-seaters, and family models with antiquated number plates and MOT stickers on windscreens. Two cars displayed out of date Road Tax licences.

Light also emanated from some of the houses, the flickering light of TV screens in front parlours, coloured light projected through the stained glass in front doors, light from bare bulbs in attic rooms where teenage girls were making up their faces or sulking after rows with their parents.

And light shone down from the walkways of Roebuck Buildings, and metropolitan luminosity overspread the scene.

Roebuck Road was not peaceful. The households of the deaf shared their TV and radio programmes with the rest of the world. Youth asserted itself with the loudness of its music, and the mothers and fathers of young people screamed and bellowed to make themselves heard. Football was being played on the asphalt pitch adjoining the car park of the Buildings, and the players shouted and cursed. Boys who had been playing kicked empty coke tins along the road as they returned home late for their tea, causing the dogs to bark.

Occasionally a car returned from a day out or one drove away: their swerving headlights and red reversing lights had dramatic effects. Not many pedestrians were about – Sunday evenings were quieter than some, and the majority of Roebuck Road residents ate their main meal, so-called tea, between six and seven. Besides, money was apt to be in short supply after Saturday evenings at The Cock in Coronation Street or bingo in Boroughfare.

The tall man striding along Roebuck Road had been a regular feature of Sunday evenings for years without number. He did not look to right or left, and never acknowledged a greeting from a stranger. He wore a brown cover-all Australian rainproof overcoat and a flat tweed cap, and carried a furled umbrella. He had a greying moustache and wore black-rimmed glasses.

He stopped at number 7, which bore the name on a metal-work plaque affixed to the garden gate, The Nest.

The small front garden was a muddle of neglected and moribund greenery. No light was visible through the windows of the house. The tall man stood by the front door and must have rung the doorbell. Immediately a light was switched on in the hall, the door opened in such a way as to hide the opener, the visitor entered and the door closed.

The person who had opened the door, the owner of the house, was a sturdy man in his sixtieth year with sparse fair hair going grey and large blue eyes. He was Robin Antrobus. The other man, who had taken off his cap but kept his mac on, was Robin's first cousin, fifty-five-year-old Maximilian Jones, called Max by his relations and few friends. They greeted each other perfunctorily, and conversed in that type of tick-tack used by members of certain families.

'Shall we go straight out?' Robin asked, and Max answered, 'If you like.'

Max replaced his cap on his full complement of iron-grey hair, and Robin reached for his camel-coloured double-breasted 'British Warm' hanging on the coat-rack in the hall, also his pork-pie hat, put them on, then asked: 'How hard is it raining?'

'Only a drizzle – you could share my brolly.'

'I'll take my stick in that case,' Robin said.

He switched off the hall light and opened the door. When he and Max were in the garden, and both had looked to see that the coast was clear, he turned a key in the mortice lock, they proceeded into the road and began to walk towards Coronation Street. Max put up his umbrella, but Robin opted to walk slightly behind him, carrying his stick – it was a defensive weapon, not an aid to walking. They did not talk, they knew where they were going. At some point Max veered across the road on to the pavement opposite and Robin followed him: they were evading a group of youths who swaggered in the direction of the Buildings, guffawing with laughter.

They negotiated Coronation Street without mishap and in Village Way headed for one of the two eateries, not the Indian restaurant and takeaway called Light of Bengal, where the spicy food upset Max's stomach, but The Zodiac, otherwise known as Ab's Caf.

It was a family business. The proprietors were the Stynes, Abraham and Miriam, Jewish cockneys, and a listless and anaemic niece, Debra, who was meant to help out. Robin with Max in tow had been a good customer over the years, and a friendly acquaintanceship had ripened little by little. They now called the Stynes by their nicknames, Ab and Mirrie, and were called Mr Robin and Mr Max – Robin had not been happy about the Misters, but Max made it clear that he wished to retain the class distinction, and Ab had had the tact to say that he had never been one to 'presume'.

The Caf had room for twelve tables with

chequered red and white paper tablecloths and a bar lined by half a dozen high stools. Ab presided behind the bar, and, on this as on other evenings, knowing the peculiarities of the two cousins, instead of greeting them in his loud voice, he smiled in their direction in an encouraging manner and pointed to their customary table in the far corner. Nine or ten people were already seated at other tables. Robin and Max sat down and studied menu cards. The food on offer seldom changed, and they knew the menu by heart, yet always read the cards as if they had never set eyes on them before. Ab, a stringy and stooping middle-aged man with a few strands of grey hair and a loose lower lip, holding a pad and pencil in one hand, came over and spoke to them.

'Gentlemen, good evening!'

He sounded more like a foreigner than a cockney, no doubt because Hebrew was his first language.

'What's it to be, Mr Robin – and what will you be drinking?'

Robin asked Max if he would like a glass of wine: he was host and would be paying for their meal.

Max said: 'Wine? That's tempting. Tell me, Ab, is the Irish stew any good?'

'Oh Mr Max,' Ab scolded, 'it's beautiful, my Mirrie was cooking it all day, she does it every Sunday, and everything's fresh here, as you know well.'

'I can't fancy anything Irish these days.'

5

'It's only a name, Mr Max – you could think it was Jewish stew.'

'Do you mean the meat's kosher?'

'It's kosher because it's good. It's not from the kosher butcher, Mr Max – I know you don't like kosher meat.'

'All right, Ab – I'm not having it anyway – I'll have the veal escalope and a glass of dry white wine.'

'One Viennese escalope and spaghetti from Milan,' Ab said, writing on his pad. 'What for you, Mr Robin?'

'I'm thinking of the boiled salt beef.'

'You wouldn't regret it – I sell buckets of salt beef.'

'Were you serving it for lunch today?'

'Oh yes, Mr Robin – many of our customers won't eat nothing else.'

'Sorry, Ab, I'll have the escalope too – but it's escalope Milanese because you serve it with spaghetti and tomato sauce – it's not Viennese at all – I've told you that before.'

'Escalope Milan,' Ab said obediently, writing on his pad. 'And drink, Mr Robin?'

'Oh' – Robin emitted a sort of long-suffering sigh – 'make mine a light ale.'

'Thank you, gents.'

Ab retreated to his position at the bar, shouted through the serving hatch in Hebrew, and prepared a tray of glasses, the wine and the light ale, and rolls and butter for Debra to carry across to the cousins' table.

The charade was over. Robin and Max always

hesitated to choose their supper and always chose exactly the same things. They all played their parts seriously, Ab included, remembered their lines and did not comment on the repetitiousness. Afterwards the cousins relaxed, they seemed to be relieved to have got through the performance, and both spoke kindly to Debra.

Robin and Max, and Max's sister Zinnia, who also lived in the Roebuck region, shared a sense of humour. It amused them, for instance, that Ab had once asked their advice about making their names sound and look less Jewish, and had then settled only on Styne rather than Stein. Ab was sure that Abraham Styne had an Anglo-Saxon ring.

Again, they saw the funny side of the escalopes they ate at the Caf. Long ago Max asked Ab if his escalope in its breadcrumbs was pork rather than the veal it purported to be, and Ab had nearly hit the roof. 'No, no, not true, Mr Max, please, you must never say that, you mustn't think it, you will get me into trouble, an escalope is a veal escalope or it's nothing, it's muck, and we don't serve you muck, Mr Max!' The cousins were co-operative. They never said the word 'pork' on the premises again. They were nonetheless tickled to think they smelt pork while they were eating veal, and that Ab was committing a religious offence for the sake of his bill of fare.

Max carved open his roll, buttered both sides, and took a large bite of one half. Robin broke his roll open by hand and began to roll bits of the soft inside into balls between his right thumb and index finger.

'How's your health?' Max inquired, munching.

'Shaky, I've been shaky,' Robin replied. 'Yours?'

'I'm still waiting for the result of my tests. I'll have to twist Scram's arm.'

Max suffered from many ailments, real or imaginary, irritable bowel syndrome, diverticulitis, inflamed duodenum and suspect gall bladder. His reference to Scram was another of the cousins' private jokes: their doctor from India was called Ram, his initials were S.C., whence the amalgamation of initials and surname.

'But have you been feeling bad?' Robin persisted.

'I never feel well.' Max stuffed buttered roll into his mouth. He chewed and swallowed and asked sharply, because he felt his almost professional invalidism was being challenged: 'What's wrong with you anyway?'

Robin flinched a little and answered: 'I'd rather not talk about it.'

Silence fell. They were accustomed to silent pauses in their conversation. This time, perhaps as usual, their speechlessness was resentful. Robin hated Max's egoism and crude manners, and Max was now feeling snubbed and was always aggravated by the fact that he was poor and dense and Robin was relatively rich and reputed to be clever.

At length Robin asked by way of compensation for having refused to pursue the subject of physical health: 'Did you go to St Mary's today?'

'I did,' said Max a trifle defensively. He and his sister were Roman Catholics, whereas Robin

8

was Church of England. Max again felt at a disadvantage because he did not belong to an English church.

'I did,' Max repeated.

'Mass?'

'Mass.'

'Did Father Murphy preach?'

'Yes – against permissiveness and immorality.'

'Was Mrs Connolly present?'

Max laughed. Mrs Connolly was a 'widow-woman', and the priest's housekeeper.

'She'd probably been absolved before the service.'

'Could well be,' Max allowed, and asked in his turn, 'Were you at St Columb's?

'I took Communion,' Robin replied, also defensively, because he was a trifle embarrassed to worship in a church dedicated to a male rather than a female saint, where the priest in charge was a respectable married man.

'Reverend Hubert officiating?' – Hubert Greenstock was the vicar.

'Yes.'

'Did he insert a sermon?'

'It was a thought for the day.'

'All church services are too long,' Max observed.

'That depends,' Robin countered.

'Think of God having to listen to them all – I pity Him!'

'He'll be pleased to know you do.'

'They're too long, that's my opinion anyway.'

'Well – we're not exactly in a tearing hurry, Max.'

9

Max flushed and refused to answer. He chose to believe that Robin was mocking his short spells of employment and long spells of unemployment. If he could have found the words, he would have cast aspersions on Robin's two slim volumes published years ago and his lifetime of so-called work on a book that was never finished.

Debra approached with a plate in each hand, a sight that always mollified Max.

Robin asked after her health: 'How are you, my dear?'

Debra shook her head from side to side, Jewish style, and, notwithstanding her rumoured addiction to recreational drugs, said: 'Good.'

She put a plate in front of each of the gentlemen and queried: 'You want any sauce at all?'

The cousins shook their heads and exchanged a look of disapproval of Debra's jargon.

'Enjoy!' she said – her parting shot.

When she was out of earshot, Max remarked as he set about his food, 'What's happened to the Queen's English?' and Robin caused them both amusement by answering ambiguously, 'Gone to pot' – a reference to marijuana.

They ate for a few minutes, then Robin said: 'Do you think this food is good for us? We've both got sensitive digestions, not to mention our diseases, and the peas aren't fresh and they're still frosty.'

'A little of what you fancy can't be bad,' Max countered.

'Well, I'm not fancying such rotten food tonight.'

'What's the problem?'

'Nothing – I've already told you I don't want to go into it.'

'Are you wanting me to eat the rest of your escalope?'

'Would you mind?'

'Hand it over.'

'I certainly will not! You'd better spear it with your fork.'

Max did so, but was clearly put out again – he felt he had been accused of lacking refinement.

Robin persisted with his spaghetti. In time he tossed another conversational ball in the air.

'How's Zinnia?'

'Fighting fit,' Max replied.

Robin almost visibly shuddered.

He said in accents of alarm: 'I'm having supper with her on Wednesday evening. I hope you're going to be there, Max. I don't want to spend hours with her if she's in her belligerent mood.'

'She hasn't invited me.'

'Couldn't you come along anyway? Shall I say that I want to see you? I could think of a reason why I need to see you.'

'She won't bite. You know she absolutely won't be interfered with.'

'That's true enough. No man's dared to interfere with her, not constructively. She's done the interfering, and look at the consequences.'

Max laughed, then added: 'You'll have to obey her – she must want you alone – but you won't get bitten if you're not for it.'

'For it? Think again! In the circumstances, three would be better company than two.'

'As a matter of fact, Robin, I won't be free on Wednesday.'

'Oh?'

'You sound surprised. I do have a social life, although you seem to be under the impression that I don't. And I do have business to attend to.'

'I'm glad to hear it.'

'New business.'

'Tell me more.'

'I'm not sure about that. I can choose to follow your example and keep my own counsel.'

'You're making me more curious, Max.'

'All right! I'm finally setting out the stall on which I have something worthwhile to sell. I admit I'm rather old for it, but taking the decision's been a tonic. And I can't wait any longer to make some money.'

'What are you doing, Max?'

'I don't like your tone, Robin. But there it is. You've always been against my projects. I'm going to offer my services as a company doctor.'

'Crumbs!'

'I'm putting an advertisement in the Friday Ad, including my qualification as a chartered accountant.'

'And your address in Roebuck Buildings?'

'That's uncalled for, Robin. I know my address isn't impressive, but the fees I shall charge will undercut other accountants.'

'Who's paying for the advert?'

'Shut up, Robin! Mind your own business. Don't forget that you're in a glass house. I may have run into difficulties with my attempts to earn my living, but your cv's worse than mine. You've just shut yourself up and lived in comfort behind the smokescreen of your scribbling. You were luckier than me, that's the only difference.'

Ab interrupted. His obsequiousness was a social lubricant. He smiled and rubbed his hands together.

'Gentlemen, food to your satisfaction?'

Robin said yes, and Max mouthed the word 'hypocrite' in his direction.

Ab was concerned.

'Mr Max, you weren't happy with the food?'

'I was as happy as usual.'

Max smiled at Ab because he was proud of his double meaning.

'Dessert, gentlemen?'

'Could I have a vanilla ice?' Robin asked.

'One vanilla ice,' Ab repeated, scribbling on his pad.

'I'll have your Peach Melba,' Max said. 'And don't write it down, Ab – we've had the same desserts for donkey's years.'

'Very good, Mr Max, very funny, Mr Max,' Ab returned, and sloped off chuckling.

Robin then handed Max an olive branch – or was it something else?

'I wonder if we should come to this place on Sunday evenings. It's quite squalid and we always seem to squabble here.'

He was spluttering. He was apt to splutter

13

when his emotions were stirred. The mobility of his upper lip got in the way of his words – he showed his upper teeth without smiling, and his tone of voice was exasperated.

Max said with provocative intent: 'There's no need to get so excited.'

'Should we try the Light of Bengal? If we want to make ourselves ill we might as well go the whole hog.'

'What's that meant to mean?'

'Oh I don't know. It doesn't matter. Here are our ices. Perhaps they'll calm us down.'

'I'm perfectly calm,' Max said.

Debra drifted across, balancing the two plates that bore the ice cream goblets. She dumped them along with another example of her gobbledegook: 'There you go!'

Max immediately dug into his Peach Melba and hummed as he ate it, indicating that it was either cold or delicious or had shocked a nerve in a tooth or had had some other effect.

Robin said: 'Sorry if I offended you.'

'Don't worry. I'm used to it. You're good to feed me as you do.'

'I'm not myself tonight.'

Max, ignoring the statement, said: 'You ought to eat that ice before it melts.'

Robin laughed, tackled his ice cream, and asked: 'What's the job of a company doctor exactly?'

'You have to restore the company to health, get it back on the rails, study the accounts, read the Riot Act, that sort of thing.'

14

'Do you charge by the hour for your services?'

'I haven't worked out my scale of fees yet. I might be paid on results.'

'Goodness! On how successful you are?'

'Right.'

'Does Zinnia know about this?'

'I haven't told Zinnia. I don't want to be discouraged by her, too.'

'It was wrong of me to be discouraging. You and I need as much encouragement as we can get. I just fear that time's running out for both of us.'

'Nonsense, Robin! You're such a pessimist. Where's your religion? You're the religious one – why not "Onward, Christian soldiers"?'

'Thanks, Max. Ill do my best. Good luck, doctor! Are you short of cash?'

'Not particularly. I'm standing on my own two feet from now on. You could invest in my business when it's up and running and before the shares are too expensive. Thank you all the same.'

'Are you sure?'

'I certainly am!'

The cousins finished their ices, and an anti-climactic silence fell. Robin drained his glass of ale, and Max dabbed his moustache with his paper napkin and sucked his teeth in a ruminant manner. Ab called to them, 'Coffee, gents?', and Robin responded by writing a bill in dumb show. When it arrived he put on his reading glasses and studied it carefully, although it seldom varied by a single penny. He paid in cash and left a tip for Debra of slightly under ten percent. The cousins stood up, Ab brought them their coats and hats, also Robin's stick and Max's umbrella, and they shook hands.

'See you next week, gentlemen,' Ab ventured to say.

The cousins replied cautiously: 'Maybe... We'll have to see... Don't expect us!'

They walked out into the Boroughfare night of speeding traffic, diesel fumes, alarming youths with raucous voices, flashing neon, music blasting from jeans shops and gales of laughter from pubs. They were too nervous to speak until they reached Coronation Street. A cat that squawked, a parked car that revved up unexpectedly, a distant firework, had had the effect of small stab wounds on the cousins.

They reached 7 Roebuck Road, The Nest.

'Do you want to come in?' Robin asked in a not very hospitable tone of voice.

'No – I'm early to bed, as you know – besides, I've a lot to do tomorrow', Max replied, suggesting he was busier than Robin.

'Oh well... Take care!'

'I will. You are a lucky chap, with your house and all. Thanks again for supper.'

They parted. Robin unlocked his front door and relocked it. He parked his stick and hung up his coat and hat without wasting electricity. He mounted the stairs, and in his bedroom he sat on the edge of the bed. Some time elapsed, and he spluttered aloud: 'Please, God, make my life worth living.'

16

2

On the Monday morning Robin Antrobus woke late, at seven-forty instead of seven o'clock. The involuntary cry he uttered after glancing at the bedside clock that had belonged to his mother expressed a variety of thoughts and emotions. He had been dreaming – it must have been another nightmare – and he was still gripped by fear and misery. Over-sleeping annoyed him: he was a creature of habit, although there was nothing much he actually had to do. He was a planner, he imposed upon himself plans or duties, and now realised that he was not going to meet his deadlines and would spend the coming day in a horrible state of haste and unpunctuality. He remembered his work; and he remembered yesterday and his unsatisfactory supper with Max. Sin crossed his mind, the sin of sloth and of malingering in bed, and by means of his groan and whimper he repulsed the feeble negativity of it, and the other negatives which had pounced on his waking.

He threw back his covers, put his pink feet on the worn Wilton carpet of the bedroom, slipped into his down-at-heel slippers, struggled into his threadbare Jaeger dressing-gown, and shuffled out and across the landing and into his bathroom with its water-heating apparatus over the brown-stained bath: he had won a minor victory and was sufficiently encouraged to proceed with his ablutions.

7 Roebuck Road was scarcely changed inside and out since it was built in the Edwardian era and bought by Robin's grandfather and inherited back in the thirties of the twentieth century by his father, Major Ronald Antrobus. Soft furnishings had come and gone, and electricity had replaced gas lighting: but a small gas fire with naked flames was still operational in the parlour on the ground floor. The architecture was simple. Parlour and dining-room were at street level; small cellar below, and kitchen down steps into extension; best bedroom and small spare on first floor with bathroom in extension; two attic rooms. The cooker and fridge were new – that is, only thirty years and twenty-odd years old respectively. The wallpapers were original inasmuch as they had survived. The brown paint on dado rails and below had also withstood the passage of time.

Robin was contrary about noise as well as other things. He hated the noisiness of Boroughfare, but also the silence of the dead of night, relative as it was in a pullulating metropolis; and again he hated the summonses to action of early morning, the scurrying footsteps of the workers of the world, the milk float's electric engine and the clinking of milk bottles, the refuse collectors' racket, and above all any lack of consideration by his neighbours. On one side of his home he had the two unmarried Padger sisters, Rhoda and Ruth, superannuated, furtive and standoffish, yet apt to move furniture about and hoover at any old hour. On the other side were the Rickitts, Bill Rickitt, a gentle soul in a somewhat monstrous body, who owned, drove and parked a juggernaut in Roebuck Road, Marge his wife who was semi-obese and loud-mouthed, and son Clay and daughter Kylie just into their teens. Robin was friendly with the Rickitts, but often disturbed by Bill's performances in his bathroom-cum-lavatory, by the foul language of Marge, and the children's screams and squabbles and perverse addiction to rock and roll.

He had a good wash, no bath, shaved and dressed in the clothes he had worn for the last few days, and went downstairs feeling guilty: he ought to have changed his pants, socks and shirt, and made his bed.

Monday morning, the first working day of the week, how it weighed upon him! The weather was brighter, was almost sunny – another disincentive to burying himself in his books.

He prepared and ate his breakfast, Corn Flakes, a slice of wholemeal bread with Anchor butter and Golden Shred marmalade, and a mug of the cheapest tea sold by the Patels in their minimarket in Coronation Street. He turned on the radio, but the news was too bad to listen to, and he switched it off again. His meal without conver-sation was a sweet and sour souvenir of the past.

His father had been that difficult type, a man

19

of few words. He died when Robin was young, thirteen years of age, but old enough to have registered the difference between home with his father in it and home with his father on active service elsewhere. Major Antrobus was large and brooding, dark, with eyebrows that were like whiskers, and unapproachable. He did well in the Second World War, achieved promotion as fellow-officers bit the dust, and met his end in the course of the Suez adventure.

It was a happy day at 7 Roebuck Road when the news of his death was received. He had scared Robin with his orders and rebukes, and losses of patience and temper; and had crushed Robin's mother. They, the survivors, celebrated their deliverance from the spell of the late unlamented by drawing still closer together. Breakfasts were never again the torturous sessions of Robin being hushed, of his mother being browbeaten, of silences broken only by sounds of the Major's teeth munching or grinding and the rustling of his newspaper.

Robin's mother's Christian name was Emily. She was the youngest of four children, whose siblings married and left her to look after their parents dying of TB. She was not a born nurse, quite the opposite, a frivolous girl who found herself trapped by circumstances. There was no escape or none that she could see: she had neither time nor opportunity to meet a wandering knight in shining armour. She was thirty when she was at last relieved of her filial obligations, a poor girl not knowing where to turn or what to do with the rest of her life. Predictably, as laid down by the law governing the way of all flesh, she then met or was found by somebody else who would victimise her. He was not a knight, but he was a soldier, and a householder with private means, ready and willing to marry and in principle protect her.

She suffered from being his wife; but perhaps she was used to suffering. She went to church in search of solace. She took her little boy to church, and she let her little boy wipe away her tears. No wonder that death exerted such a powerful influence on both Emily and Robin! It had twice come to her rescue, and once, already, to his.

A period without history, a happy period in Robin's memory, ensued. He grew up and remained a mother's boy. But too soon Emily, dogged by a new fear, resorted to the blackmail of ill-health to stop her son straying from her side.

It was not much of a hardship so far as he was concerned. He could have done without the worry of her ailments and pain, but was passive, unadventurous sexually, not of a romantic disposition, dependent on her and her financial resources, and had work to do, a vocation to work in his chosen field. His comfort and consolation after she had passed over was that he had not let her down.

Now, sitting at the kitchen table, he ate his traditional breakfast, as if to confirm that he was not repudiating his past.

Robin was a committed Christian – being a Christian had saved him from perhaps being nothing – and the sentence that had been his motto through the ups and more precisely the downs of his sixty years was, 'Thy will be done'.

He picked up the newspaper on the kitchen table. It was a tabloid – he had bought it yesterday in Tesco's, hoping no one had seen him doing so. He extracted his spectacles from his top pocket, polished the lenses with his handkerchief, and put them in position: he could read fairly well without specs but used them for his close work, and he wanted to get a good clear view of the photographs. He peered at the topless model on the inside page with interest but without excitement: he was intrigued by the prices that had been paid by Adam and his male descendants for the services rendered by Eve and her daughters. Why was the female form so valuable? What was so wonderful about its little differences from masculinity? He was too old to unearth the answers to such riddles, and he knew in his heart that the mysteries he sought to penetrate in his work were of greater weight and importance, at least intellectually.

The reminder of work made him read the news from the nation's gutters. At length his guilt got the better of him, he attended to household chores, and at about ten o'clock, bracing himself, entered his workroom, the old parlour, and pulled back the moth-eaten red plush curtains.

The scene brought him out in a sweat. Most

of the original furniture was in the dining-room, piled in there anyhow, the settee on top of the dinner-table, the easy chairs on the sideboard, the upright piano almost blocking entry and pictures stacked on the floor. The dining-room was a lost cause, the realm of spiders, just as the parlour was the realm of books. A plasterer's table on trestles, a two-metre plank of wood-type material, filled the central space. Major Ron's desk stood in the window, his large armchair at the other end of the room against the wall, and harder chairs were scattered about, some old, others modern secretarial swivellers. But every level surface was covered with books. They were on the mantelpiece, the chairs, the desk, the central table and extra folding card tables. Books camouflaged the furnishings. Books gathered dust and made the room smell musty. Books combined with the thick net curtains to steal the light.

Robin stood by the plasterer's table, taking deep breaths with difficulty.

He did not sit down, he was afraid to, if he had sat he would have been under pressure to work. He read the title of his life's work on the top page of twenty-five centimetres of typescript, *The Analogical Review of Religions*, and his breaths were shallower and faster – his breathing had become one of the main causes of his writer's block. His panic attacks, the sweating and breathlessness would be the end of his story, he feared, his book and probably himself. He had to give in, he had to leave the room, and he did so, slamming the door behind him.

How feeble! How ridiculous! He jeered at his over-reaction to the strain of authorship. But his conscience reminded him that he had been writing the *Analogical Review* for thirty-odd years, writing and not writing it, and that his literary ineffectiveness was shameful, although charity might call it tragic. He recalled his mother's high hopes and her conviction that he would be famous, and was half-glad that she was not alive to be disappointed by his failure. He could almost hear his father calling him idle and lackadaisical.

He left the house. He needed fresh air. He needed to escape. He seized his British Warm, hat and stick, stood under his porch, refilling his lungs, valuing his freedom however temporary, checking that no one and nothing threatened him in the street, and locked his front door. He might be craven, and by no means for the first time, but it was not a crime to try to regain his composure, and after all he could afford to pretend he was a gentleman of leisure.

Money was Robin's lifeline. Ever since he had lost his mother, he had been supported by his statements from bank and building society, and by his cheque book – he did not dare to have a credit or debit card. He had inherited more than enough to cover his expenses, and the old age pension shed a rosy light across the future. His father had been one of two children, son and daughter of a well-to-do dealer in and restorer of antique furniture. Major Ron's sister, Irene, had married Julius Jones, a drifter and wastrel, who ran through most of her inheritance.

There was never inclination on the richer side of the family to hand over the differential to the poorer. Major Ron considered his sister a halfwit and her husband, his brother-in-law Julius, a parasite; Emily, Major Ron's wife and heiress, was not going to give anyone a penny that might be of use to their son; and Robin not only treasured her money that became his, but was determined not to pour down an open drain any of the means to the end of his literary endeavours. He knew that Max and Zinnia thought he was tight-fisted, and that their resentment was a feature of their friendship with himself. He also knew, had always known, that Max was lazy and a money-grubber, and that Zinnia, who was sharp and a good earner, could have helped her brother more than she ever did.

Robin headed for his bank in Coronation Street. He would ask for the balance of his account, which usually boosted his confidence and was actually health-giving, and he might indulge in a visit to his building society for the same reason.

Unfortunately St Columb's Church was located not far from his bank. Robin hoped not to meet the vicar, Hubert Greenstock, who took an intrusive interest in his writing. He was loath to have to gulp out the refrain that he had made no progress since he was last questioned. Hubert was a decent man, Hubert was all very well, but Robin wished he was at the bottom of the sea. He retracted it – his conscience smote him – he prayed subliminally to be forgiven his trespass

– and realised with a shock that his thoughts had been unpardonably materialistic in a sort of spiritual zone.

Memories and comparisons seemed to catch up with him and tug at his sleeve. He had been a religious prodigy. He seemed to be one of the children blessed by Jesus, and was expected to become a noted minister of the church or an inspiring theologian. He loved his religion, was uplifted by church services and Bible Class – at first he associated his tribulations as the son of his father with those of Jesus, and then he sought the absolution promised by holy texts for his sin of being pleased that Major Ron was dead. St Columb's was not avoided in those days, it was the refuge of his youth and his inadequacies at school.

He still glowed with religion in his early manhood. His favourite reading was the lives of saints who had abjured worldly pleasure and mostly come to sticky ends. In his twenties he wrote *A Prayer a Day*, a brief account of his own religious observances, its title deriving from the old rhyming recipe for health, an apple a day keeps the doctor away. It had a success in the circles of the pious, and sold reasonably well in the houses of God. He followed it up with *Faith Wallops Logic*, which was a mistake from start to finish: the title caused misgivings and offence, the argument that Christianity was not and did not need to be rational was heresy, and the potentates of the Synod banned the book from their bookstalls. Robin had written it in his one and only almost manic interval, when higher spirits had ruled and he had felt entitled to lay down his law.

He cringed to remember it. His reaction to adverse criticism had lasted for years. Kind people, literary people, had doled out encouragement, and some had begged him to undertake a bigger better book, thence *The Analogical Review*; but he had begun it without much confidence, had lost more confidence the more he appreciated the size of the task he had set himself, and his innate diffidence, timidity, tendency to get depressed, and low blood pressure had put spoke after spoke in the wheel of the enterprise.

These days, these darkening November days, his religion offered less and asked for more. He pleaded for mercy, almost as cousin Max pleaded that he was poor. It was not fair: he wanted the Almighty to solve his problem for no fee. He thought of looking into St Columb's after all; but was deterred by the selfishness of the prayer he would offer up, not to mention the attentions of Hubert Greenstock.

He proceeded into Village Way, and was brought down to earth by the smell of food emanating from Ab's Caf and the kebab shop. He had intended to buy his lunch and other eatables from the Patels, but was afraid he would have to enter into conversations there. On impulse he stepped on to a bus at the bus-stop that was going to the Tesco's in Boroughfare.

He was never unhappy in Tesco's. He could feast his eyes on the goods in the shelves and dodge people he knew or who knew him in the aisles. He bought a mild curry meal for one, some slices of ham, cheese, bread and apples, and walked home with a bulging bag in each hand and his stick hooked in a top pocket of his coat.

At 7 Roebuck Road he cooked and ate lunch, then was overcome by sleepiness. He was tempted and yielded to temptation, mounted the stairs, lay down on his bed and slept for two solid hours. He stirred and again renewed his resolution not to pass out like that in the afternoons. He went downstairs, made and drank a cup of tea, and, marching purposefully into his front room, switched on the lights and drew the curtains.

He did not quail before his work in progress at this time of day. Being there with curtains excluding ordinary life was more bearable than morning sunshine and people in Roebuck Road visibly marching to and fro with enthusiasm. He glanced at a page of manuscript, opened a book, and began to copy something in the book on to a new piece of A4 paper in a pad. He was adding to his list of the twenty-two thousand different churches and sects of the worldwide Protestant communion.

He graduated to a more scholarly challenge. Why was it that Jesus referred to God, His Father, by the Aramaic word 'abba', unusual in religious discourse in Judaism, and as a rule employed by the children of Jews talking to their earth-father and meaning, in English, 'daddy'? Robin knew that Aramaic was a semitic language, but did not understand it or its usage. His lack of knowledge went annoyingly deeper. While it was sweet of Jesus to speak publicly of His Daddy, was it respectful, could it have pleased the scribes and pharisees, and would it not have been sneered at by the academics in their hoity-toity manner? For decades he had puzzled over such questions, and, try as he would and had done, had so far failed to find an analogical link between the founder of Christianity, who spoke to the God in heaven in the terms of childish innocence, and the founder of Islam, whose interest in commerce and his military leadership were extremely grown-up.

Robin delved yet again into the encyclopedias, the Bibles and the Koran, the histories, biographical and theological texts he had bought long ago, when he was more hopeful of bringing his *magnum opus* to a successful conclusion. Scepticism as to the outcome of his research notwithstanding, he did manage to lose himself in the familiar maze of scholarship. Perhaps, he reflected at one moment, research was more like hunting than getting lost: a fact or a date was the quarry, and he was the modern intellectual version of the hunter-gatherer of his primordial ancestry, chasing through the forest of the relevant material on offer and tracking down and closing in for the kill.

He glanced at his wristwatch, which was dainty and had belonged to his mother. The time was nearly eight. He deserved to call it a day. Thankfully, he adjourned to the kitchen and made himself a sandwich with the Tesco ham, and switched on the TV. He zapped as he ate, watching now a quiz, then a whodunit, followed by a news, a political bout that was almost fisti-cuffs, and a Hollywood film. He was inattentive, nothing made much impression on him, his mind was otherwise engaged, he had reverted to thinking about himself.

His difficulty on this Monday that was ending better than it had begun was, in a word, Max. The ember of dissatisfaction that had smouldered for most of his life was bursting into the flame of rebellion. Max's friendship was false, he poured cold water on Robin's literary efforts, studied to patronise his elder and better cousin even as the latter entertained him to supper in restaurants, and had cast a blight over Robin's whole existence. He was the vampire who had sucked the blood of Robin's creativity. He was taller, a stronger personality, gloomier with reason, and poorer: he was wrong in every respect. The time had come for a final break, for adieu. Without Max hanging round his neck, he might learn to fly again in existential and literary senses.

Robin paused in his inner argumentation. He shunned what was clear cut, he favoured the fuzzy edge. He remembered his other cousin, Zinnia, who was younger and cleverer than Max, presented a range of further difficulties, and with whom he was dining on the day after tomorrow. He could not stifle a retrograde wish that Max might be invited by his sister.

3

At seven o'clock on the Wednesday evening he 'dressed for dinner', his phrase indicating that he had a bath and another partial shave, discarded the socks, pants and shirt he had worn for more days than he could remember and put on replacements, tied a tie round his neck, wetted and combed his hair, and was ready for the fray.

Downstairs he donned his British Warm and pork-pie, armed himself with his stick, stole out of the house, surveyed the road to right and left, and, having decided that hostile forces were not about, scuttled down the garden path on to the pavement. He walked to Coronation Street, turned right, passed St Columb's, and turned right again into Coronation Close, an estate of a dozen two-storey private dwellings built in the 1950s, in number 8 of which Zinnia lived. He rang the doorbell and waited.

The house had been bought by his aunt, Irene Jones, née Antrobus. She lived there with husband Julius when he felt like it, brought up their two children under its pantile roof, resolutely refused to mortgage it in order to raise money for her husband or her son to spend, and stayed put as a widow and died in her own marital bed. Her daughter Zinnia had never left home. It was not exactly for want of trying: she almost married several men and was often a bridesmaid reluctantly. But she was dutiful, and fond of her mother. She trained as a secretary and landed her perennial job as receptionist in the offices of Watkins and Hillingdon, solicitors in Highgate, and PA to David Hillingdon. She earned money and contributed to the expenses of 8 Coronation Close. She was rewarded by becoming its sole owner – Max was left most of the family money, which he lost.

Now, Zinnia could be heard treading heavily on the tiles of the hallway. She switched on an interior light and another dazzling security light in the porch, flung the front door wide open and stood in the embrasure, filling it.

She was a six-footer, big-boned and stout, with a large-featured face and wiry iron-grey hair that was cut short and in a man's style. She had a wide smile, lipstick all over her lips, protruding upper front teeth, and her voice boomed.

She boomed Robin's name by way of greeting and held out her arms preparatory to embracing him. He took off his cap and submitted – as usual, she squeezed him until he was breathless and actually lifted him over the lintel.

'Robin!' she repeated, laughing and slamming the front door. 'Come in – let me have your weapon – disrobe, please – here, I'll take off the overcoat – come into my parlour!'

Her words were either ill-chosen or deliberately suggestive, Robin never knew which. He followed her – crawled after her like a fly – into the brightly-lit lounge-cum-dining-room.

Max was not there. Robin was the more alarmed.

He ventured to ask: 'Is your brother joining us?'

'What do we want with silly old Max playing gooseberry?' she replied with a flirty look. 'Drink, Robin – what's yours? I'm all behind – no, don't laugh, no pun intended – I'm only just back from the office.' And she launched into conventional lamentations about her boss – 'Selfish man, typical man, wants too much of me!' – and London Transport, while opening and shutting drawers in the sideboard and slapping down eating irons and glasses on the dining-table. 'But you haven't told me what you want to drink. I've some sweetish white in the fridge – would that do?' He nodded and would have spoken, but she exclaimed: 'Okay, let's hit the bottle. I'm still cooking, incidentally – you'll have to wait to get your greens.' She grinned at him again before striding into the kitchen.

Robin sat down on an armchair, not on the sofa, where she might join him. His fear of Zinnia went back a long way. Once nearly forty years ago, at a Christmas party in a large house inhabited by a girlfriend of Zinnia and her wealthy family, they were all playing Sardines, the cousins hid together in a cramped cupboard, and she kissed him. He had nightmares because of it – he had felt like Jonah being swallowed by the whale. Ever since, he had avoided

33

circumstances that could be considered intimate by Zinnia, had steered well clear so far as was possible because of the family entanglement, and she had taunted and teased him.

'How are you, Robin?' she called from the kitchen, and, before he could tell her truthfully as well as defensively that he had been feeling pretty bad, she continued: 'You're looking quite bonny.'

He experienced a pang of hatred of her, but smiled when she lumbered in bearing wine in cloudy wine glasses.

And she did not improve matters by raising her glass to him and saying with a wink: 'Bottoms up!'

They drank the cloying liquid. She then instructed him to sit at his place at the table and returned to the kitchen, where she clattered pots and pans, cursed, hummed tunelessly as if to prove she was enjoying herself whether or not he was, and occasionally shouted upsetting items of news: 'I hope to God this pâté hasn't gone off... Oh Lord, now I've cut my finger and there's blood everywhere.'

Robin asked himself: 'Why am I here?' He crossed his arms, he shrank into a self-embrace, groaned answers to which she did not listen, and yearned for The Nest or any place which was not the lair of his maneater of a hostess.

At last she emerged from the kitchen, placed on the table a rack of limp triangles of toast with the crusts on and a plastic container half full of chicken liver pâté with brandy.

'Dig in,' she ordered, and he obeyed.

The pâté was tasty, he had to admit, but he only finished eating his portion with difficulty after remembering that rotten meat was said to be tastier than the fresh sort.

The conversation began by Robin mentioning his Sunday supper with Max.

She asked: 'Ab's Caf again?'

'Yes.'

'You two are so original.'

'He likes it there.'

'You both must, you've eaten there for long enough. What did Max have to say for himself?'

Robin hedged: 'When did you last have words with him, Zinnia?'

'I don't know – the other day – what's up? Is he ill, or doing something different as per usual?'

'He's decided to be a company doctor.'

'A what?'

Robin gave her a full account of his exchange with Max, and she reacted in line with her legal background.

'A company doctor, that's false pretences or anyway against the Trade Descriptions Act. I'll squeeze a ruling out of my *Maitre* Hillingdon.' She often slapped the prefix of French lawyers on to her bosses' names. 'As for my brilliant brother, he's going to get himself locked up before we know where we are. Of course, *he's* never known where he is. Mercy me, talk of a fertile brain – he should be taking the contraceptive pill!'

They clucked together – Max's aberrations were always a bond of sorts between them.

35

Robin inquired: 'Have you any idea of the costs involved in setting up as a company doctor?'

'And what about liabilities?'

'I suspect the financial crunch will come when he's advised a company to be bankrupt.'

'Don't frighten me, Robin.'

'Well, to start with, he spoke of advertising his services. And he'll be needing stationery and so on. I think he's spent money already, and I've wondered where he got it.'

'Not from me. I wouldn't back any more of his bright ideas. There's that friend of his in Roebuck Buildings, the widow, Mrs Withers, poor old cow, he's milked her before and probably this time round.'

They were amused by Zinnia's turn of phrase and shared a giggle.

She continued: 'One thing's certain, there'll be a bill at the end of the doctor's day, and we'll be paying it, or you will mostly.'

Robin stiffened.

'Oh no, Zinnia, you're labouring under a misapprehension.'

'Don't be funny, Robin, labouring under a misapprehension – talk English, for goodness sake!'

'Very well, I'm not paying a penny more for Max's brainwaves – brainstorms, I should say.'

'Have you told him?'

'What? No, but I will. The fact is, I've more than that to tell him. I don't want to see Max any more.'

'Have you quarrelled?'

'It's nothing to do with quarrelling, although I do detest his huffiness. He's not good for me, he's really bad for my character, he depresses and irritates me – I can't work for ages after our Sunday evenings – it's high time, Zinnia, it really is!'

'Oh dear!'

She spoke annoyingly, as if to a child, a child not taken seriously, with a mixture of comfort and mockery.

While he searched in vain for a crushing retort, she pushed back her chair, stacked their plates, and made for the kitchen.

'Help yourself to the plonk,' she shouted in her indelicate lingo.

Their next course was frozen stew, available from the Patels' minimarket, and now served in its individual plastic containers, one on each of their plates. To go with it were microwaved green beans and outsize chips.

Zinnia emptied the contents of her container on to her plate, and urged Robin to follow her example. He did so and burned his fingers on the plastic – what were her fingers made of? She then stacked the two containers and tossed them into the waste paper basket by her desk – a WPB was not a sanitary receptacle. They began to eat again.

Zinnia raised her head, as if from the trough, and remarked: 'You won't cut Max out of your life completely, will you?'

'In principle, yes.'

'You're not chickening out because he might cost you money in the future?'

'No, I'm not.'

'But you are a tightwad, Robin.'

'That's unfair. I've subsidised Max. I've done my best. Please don't be nasty to me – I must give my work a chance. Max is an obstacle between me and getting my book finished. You don't understand, or you won't. I'm nearly sixty and must finish my book now or never.'

'Oh yes, your book!'

'Please, Zinnia!'

Robin would not look at her. He dropped his eyes, as the saying goes, and stared into his stew. He was conscious of his heart beating and not beating – it seemed to be missing beats – he was invariably agitated by the dismissive attitude of people to his writing. He hoped she was not going to call him a sluggard and layabout, and that, if or when she did so, he would not crumple completely.

He stole a glance at her from under his eyebrows. He had been surprised by her un-characteristic silence. He saw her huge hands holding knife and fork on either side of her plate as if in suspended animation. She had a blood-stained tuft of cotton wool on the ball of the thumb of her left hand. In spite of having been ready to kill her a moment or two ago, he asked if she was all right.

Her response was acrimonious.

'I'm never not all right.' She loaded her fork and stuffed food into her mouth. 'But I do wish you wouldn't harp on age. I don't like it.'

'There's no alternative to being the age we are.'

'Oh Robin, you're a prig too! It's all right for you, being sixty, you can afford to do as you please and lurk in your hermitage.'

'Well, you're not poor – you can't be.'

'By the time Max has finished with me I'll be on the breadline. You won't help him, and I bet you wouldn't help me.'

'I haven't said I wouldn't help you,' Robin protested, and bit his tongue.

'Thank you, cousin. I'll believe it when I see it, but thanks for the kind thought. You're not the only one who's misunderstood. I'll have to retire soon – my bosses have kept me on longer than they absolutely needed to. How I'll manage without an office to go to, and colleagues and my salary, I do not know.'

'I'm sure, Zinnia...'

She interrupted him.

'Oh yes, you're sure, everybody is, except me. But I'm a practical person, and I've still got a twinkle in my eye. I could do a lot for a man, and to him, I've bags of experience, and somebody who knew which side his bread was buttered wouldn't regret me. Do you catch my drift, Robin? Don't look so shifty! Have you had enough to eat?'

His heart had developed another worrying symptom, it had sunk throughout Zinnia's speech, which was delivered with sideways glances and even a wink at himself. In answer to her question, he swallowed his final mouthful whole, without chewing it, storing up indigestion for later, and answered in a rush that he had had enough,

39

more than enough, an involuntary reference to her flirting.

'Couldn't you squeeze in an ice?'

He hesitated, and cursed himself for his hesitancy.

'I bought you your favourite strawberry ice.'

'Well, a little, thank you.'

'How many balls?'

He jumped: was she being vulgar?

'One, please.'

'You disappoint me, Robin.'

She laughed, stacked plates and carried them into the kitchen.

He suffered from a feeling that things were going from bad to worse, and loosened his tie and undid the top button of his shirt, hoping his perspiration was not visible.

The ice she brought him was the ripple variety, with a darker pink line or two running through it. Robin cooled himself with a taste and asked Zinnia a question about her next year's holiday, traditionally the topic of conversation she liked best. She described the coach-tour of the Scottish highlands in the month of May she had booked. She listed the places she would see and stay in, and was glad to say she was not being overcharged.

'What are Scotsmen like?' she asked.

'Dour,' Robin replied.

'Is it true that they don't wear knickers under their kilts?'

'Really, Zinnia!'

'I'll get the coffee.'

He had been lulled into a sense of false security

by her monologue. He now scented danger, and his nerves resumed their jangling.

She re-entered bearing a tray laid with a percolator, a silver cream jug, a sugar basin, two cups, two small glasses filled with brown liquid, and a dish of chocolate mints, and headed for the coffee table in front of the sofa.

'Come and sit over here,' she said, 'we'll be more comfortable.'

Robin thought: speak for yourself, but obeyed her.

They sat side by side on the sofa, and she served him in such a cosseting manner that the comparison of a domestic creature being fattened up for slaughter crossed his mind.

'What's in the glasses, Zinnia?'

'Something special.' She lifted one glass and raised it in his direction. 'Here's to you, Robin!'

'You must tell me what it is.'

'Try it – you'll love it – clink glasses with me!'

'Oh very well,' he allowed ungraciously.

'Not a sip, Robin, a gulp. Be brave!'

'Here's to you, Zinnia!'

He tossed it back, thinking of Socrates and the hemlock, and was left with a whiskyish taste in his mouth. At least he was fairly sure it had not been poison.

Yes, it was whisky, Zinnia told him, Japanese whisky that was stronger than Scotch.

His simmering hatred of her bubbled up. Now she had her hand on his thigh. He was much too old for her bullying and Japanese whisky.

'How are you really, Robin?' she asked.

'I'm not unwell,' he replied and blushed on account of the double negative. 'Or well,' he added.

'Aren't you ever lonely? I'm going to be lonelier still when I'm not working. And if I have to fork out for Max yet again I'll be rat-poor into the bargain.'

'You don't have to fork out for Max. Let him sink or swim for a change.'

'He'll force me to give him my money.'

'I can't believe anyone's succeeded in forcing you to do anything you didn't want to do.'

'You're so wrong about me, Robin. You always have been. I know I look big and strong, but I'm terribly sensitive underneath. You'd find out if you gave me the benefit of the doubt.'

'Zinnia, I don't know what this is all about.'

'It's about you and me.'

'Oh no!'

'Don't be like that! Keep calm for a change. We should have got together years ago – think of the money and trouble we would have saved between us! It's not marriage I'm after – I'm sick of sex – and it isn't security. It's companionship.'

'Zinnia,' he said repressively, squirming on the sofa and reaching for his spectacles in his jacket pocket.

'Don't stop me, hear me out,' she said, and then: 'Why are you putting your specs on? I like you better without them.'

'I need them, I feel I need them, that's why.'

'You've put them on for protection.'

42

'No, I haven't.'

'Okay – as you please – I don't mind. If I go bankrupt, Robin, you would take me in, wouldn't you?'

'But you're not bankrupt, and I'm not making promises I might not be able to keep.'

'It's mean of you, you know.'

'No, it isn't. The truth is I'm not well, not at all, and I might have to sell my house to raise money to keep me in an eventide home. And if I wasn't an invalid when you thought of moving in, I'd have to have solitude for my work.'

'I'd let you do your work, but solitude's not good for anybody. I'd cheer you up and show you a bit of life with a capital L.'

'It's out of the question, Zinnia. I'm sorry to say so, but, frankly, you shouldn't have proposed yourself to be at least my guest for life. You'd be a cuckoo in my Nest with a vengeance.'

They both had to laugh at his witticism.

But she resumed: 'I wish you'd explain your blasted old book to me. I know it's bound to be miles above my head, but why exactly is it so important for you and the world in general?'

'Are you scoffing again? You and Max have always scoffed at it.'

'I haven't, I've never talked to you about it, but I can't answer for Max. Truly, Robin, I'd be interested.'

'I don't discuss it, I can't, writers write, they don't talk their writing.'

'Why is it taking so much time?'

'Because the subject's so vast. It's a comparison

of the religions of the human race reaching back to the year dot.'

'How awful!'

'The subject could defeat me.'

'You couldn't let such a thing happen, not after all your work.'

'No – well – that's why I don't want to be interrupted or distracted.'

'Why on earth didn't you choose a normal career, Robin?'

'You've forgotten, or perhaps never knew, how religious I was when I was young.'

'Past tense?'

'No – I still am. I was explaining that I decided to do the big book after my two short religious books were published.'

'I'd forgotten them.'

'People have forgotten.'

'Do you love your writing?'

'Not when I'm blocked.'

'Blocked?'

'I've had writer's block for a few years – I can't actually write much – but I do research that would be useful when I get the writing under way.'

'When's that? And how does it happen?'

'By luck, by patience – no one knows for sure.'

'Robin, should you go to a psychiatrist?'

'No, Zinnia...'

'A psychiatrist might help you with our relationship. You might learn how to love somebody properly, a woman, or even a man.'

Robin stood up. He was shaking. He was spluttering.

'No, no, you're not to try to reorganise my life to suit yourself – you're a meddler – good night!'

'Don't be a silly boy, a silly old boy – sit down,' she was saying.

'Where are my things?'

'Don't run away!'

'I won't listen to your nonsense, Zinnia. Give me my coat!'

'Robin, we'd get on perfectly well if you weren't so touchy and were more co-operative.'

'Where's my stick? Oh, thank you. Thanks for dinner. How do I get out of this door?'

'Kiss me good night!'

'Oh Zinnia!'

He turned his head to one side. She could not reach his mouth, but she butted her head against his cheekbone.

He was finally in the fresh air. He felt like Lazarus. His heart began to regain its rhythm, his blood reached his extremities. 7 Roebuck Road, the mirage of it, danced before his eyes, and the mental picture of his front room was a view of heaven.

He walked homewards. But habitual anxieties now took over from those from which he was escaping. Two young black boys were lounging about at the corner of Coronation Street. He gritted his teeth and approached them, taking a firmer hold of his stick, and stumbled and fell on his knees.

45

The black boys helped him to his feet. They asked if he was all right. He sobbed out an affirmative and hurried on. They had not stolen his wallet. He could not stop sobbing quietly. It had been a bad evening. He was not in a good state physically, mentally or morally. He was in the wrong too often. He should be dead, he wished he was for about the hundredth time. To make matters worse or possibly better, he recollected Zinnia's ice. He suspected that the ripple effect, the darker pink lines, were actually streaks of blood from her thumb.

4

Robin's night was bad. He could not get to sleep
for rueing his acceptance of Zinnia's invitation
to dinner, and for smarting under her charge
that he was a psychiatric case. When he went
to sleep he had nightmares in which he was
bound, chained, about to be tortured and shot.
In the small hours of the morning he had reason
to believe that the pâté was to blame for his
suicidal inclinations. And between four-thirty and
six-thirty he was nauseated by the idea that he
had consumed the blood of Zinnia.

Six-thirty was when Robin's neighbours stirred.
He liked the Rickitts, and so long as he was
sleeping or had slept well he did not notice their
noise. But on this Thursday morning, because
he was worn out, his nervous system took grave
exception to Bill yawning, belching, passing water
and wind, groaning on the lavatory and singing
in the bath in his bathroom next door. Then
Marge yelled 'Wakey wakey' at the children and
called them most of the names under the sun,
and soon the pop music seemed to rattle Robin's
rafters.

Similarly, although he was quite fond of Ruth
and Rhoda Padger, he objected to the disturbances

they were making so early in the day. They seemed to be bumping a clothes cupboard down the stairs and simultaneously slamming doors: how was it possible?

Church would be more peaceful than home. Church was again a straw to clutch at. He was wide awake, too upset to sleep or work, and St Columb's offered Communion at eight o'clock on every weekday. He might as well go to it. He rephrased his decision apprehensively: he was glad he could spare the time to seek solace in the house of God. He put on yesterday evening's tie, and accoutred himself in his outdoor winter clothes.

He walked briskly to St Columb's. Businessmen and office workers had no time to stare at him. It was too early for the unemployed and those being cared for in the community to scare him in one way or another. A few school children were already traipsing to school, and doubtless a few truants were not.

He was not an ardent churchgoer. He refused to be a church mouse. He was apt to be bored by Matins and was definitely depressed by Evensong. The Communion Service was preferable to the other two. And he had to be grateful to Hubert Greenstock for refusing to use the New English Bible and sticking to the old poetic version.

He entered the Victorian building and tiptoed to his customary pew. Dawn was breaking and illuminating the coarse stained-glass portrait of Jesus in the eastern window. Robin bowed his head in prayer; but he kept on thinking of Zinnia's unforgivable trespasses. Hubert in white surplice and pop art tabard swept in, followed by the youth with learning difficulties who was attempting to master the duties of acolyte, and the service began.

Robin apologised to God for his inattention. The dozen other members of the congregation were nearly all female and older than he was. Mrs Caudle with her chesty cough was still alive, but Miss Woodly, a bag of bones muffled up in scarves, looked as if she was half through death's door. Robin flinched squeamishly at Hubert's consecration of the bread and wine, representing the body and blood of the Saviour. He was the first to kneel at the altar rail, the others had difficulty in getting there and could not kneel; and he felt sick without warning when he partook of what was in the chalice. He returned to his seat, meaning to stay until the service was finished. But somehow he could not. He had mingled in his mind the blood of Zinnia and of Jesus; and was afraid that he might vomit or cry, and had to be on his own.

He stole out, eyes down.

Was he iller than he had thought he was?

He remembered Max. He and Zinnia had discussed both Max's career – his career downhill, it could have been said – and his health, which was poor in fact as well as in a fictional sense. Robin could do with sympathy in the storm of one sort or another that seemed to be gathering over his head; yet he had dealt with Max

49

unsympathetically. He was bored by Max's tribulations, yet fascinated by his own. How unfair! Why was everything a muddle?

He stood indecisively in Coronation Street. He was circumscribed by regrets and enemies: that was how he felt. He was also hungry, he had had no breakfast. He walked towards Boroughfare purposefully.

There was a café in Boroughfare, a rough place with permanently steamed up windows, nothing like Ab's Caf that presumed to be a restaurant. It was called Florrie's and was next door to the Surgery of the doctors' practice of which Scram was a member. Robin could kill two birds with one stone, get something to eat at Florrie's and consult Dr Ram – and he hoped his own death in person would not choose to feature in the programme.

Florrie's was packed, he had to share a table with a tramp – a proper tramp with matted beard and itches, not the modern drugged beggar type – who drank tea out of his saucer and guzzled a bacon sandwich. Some liquid was spilt on the table top, an ashtray had fag-ends in it, a radio blared and common voices were raised: Robin's mood was suited by the idea that he was plumbing the lower depths. He would have been nervous on any other day, now he was uncaring.

Nobody took his order. The tramp, when Robin asked how to get food, pointed with his thumb at the bar, behind which presumably Florrie, large and hot, presided. He approached her and ordered tea and toast, and she called him 'Guvnor'. Then, standing by the bar, he was aware of hostile stares, and realised that he had stumbled into the class war, and could not flee into classlessness and anonymity.

He carried his mug and plate to his table. The tramp had gone, but nobody took the empty chair although customers were crowding in. Robin was discriminated against and sadder than ever, and, regardless of indigestion, bolted his toast surely spread with marge. He escaped from Florrie's and entered the reception area of the Surgery.

It was empty. Robin was glad to be first in, but vaguely perturbed to reflect that a doctor without patients was unlikely to be a good one.

Dr Ram emerged from his consulting room in the manner of mine host. He was small and tubby, balding and with a sweet easy smile. He called Robin by his Christian name while Robin called him Scram: they were friends and had worked out how to address each other.

'What have you brought me today, Robin?' he inquired in a rallying tone of voice.

Robin shook his head and Scram's hand, and they adjourned into the latter's consulting room and sat on either side of a desk with a computer on it and a photograph of Mrs Ram and some little Rams.

'Tell me your troubles now.'

Robin tried to correct the teasing intonation. 'I'm ill.'

'In what portion of your anatomy has the illness struck?'

'I seem to be breaking down everywhere and in every sense.'

'That is not perfect. It can hardly be worse than you describe. What are the symptoms?'

'I have no resistance to stress. I must have the lowest blood pressure and the slowest recovery rate of anybody who appears to be alive.'

'You have not lost your sense of humour, Robin.'

'It's no joke.'

'Shall we have a look at you?'

'I wish we would.'

Scram sniggered and asked Robin to strip to the waist.

'How is the book?'

'In a bad state, too.'

'Ah!'

'No – I'm not ill because the book's in trouble, it's the other way round.'

'We shall see. As you know, Robin, I would like to have been a writer. Unfortunately my wife would not have liked it – she is a hungry woman and expects to have food on the table for herself and her children.'

'Aren't they your children?'

'I believe so. I hope so. I am a happily married man, Robin, and determined to remain so. On the other hand, it would have suited me to dawdle by a river writing poetry.'

'My writing's nothing like that.'

'Sit here and lend me your arm. Agreed, my writing would be different from yours. It would be more of a sexual and commercial nature. Your blood pressure is high.'

52

'You surprise me.'

'What will your heart whisper to me? Deep breaths, if you would be so kind.'

After a pause Scram removed his stethoscope and said: 'Your heart is misbehaving, Robin. It is not in a good mood. Show me your tongue! Any unusual developments in the bowel area or the waterworks department? Sleep pattern normal?'

'I feel I'm dying, Doctor.'

'You are, so am I, and your death may be imminent, I cannot assure you that it is not, but, medically speaking, you are not ready to leave us. I will give you a prescription and make an appointment for you with a cardiac specialist.'

'I feel I'm losing my grip.'

'Is it the book?'

'I'm afraid I may never finish it.'

'Sorry, I have no pills for that condition. However, there is a saying that art is a cry of fear.'

'I'm not a real literary artist, I'm another sort of writer, a religious writer, a would-be religious historian, but in fact I no longer know what I am. I think I'm just nothing.'

'You are wrong, but you will say I am obliged to diagnose that you are something and you do have a future. Would you wish to consult a psychotherapist or even a psychiatrist?'

'You're the second person to talk to me about psychiatry in the last twenty-four hours. No! I'm not a lunatic.'

'You use a taboo word – please lower your voice or I will be thrown into the dungeons for permitting its use. I meant only that you have anxieties that could be eased by professional means.'

'Goodbye, Scram – and I'm sorry to have kept you so long.'

Robin began to put on his clothes.

Scram said: 'My prescription will help you. I give it to you on the understanding that you will not embarrass me by taking precipitate action.'

'I won't kill myself, I'm too cowardly to do such a thing.'

'Cowardice saves lives. Come back to talk to me when we hear from the specialist. My advice to you is chin up, Robin.'

'Thank you.'

Robin went to Tesco's. His dissatisfaction with Scram was modified by the pleasure of finding himself again in that treasure house. It took him back to shopping with his mother: he had loved shops then – he saw the stuff for sale as presents or prizes he might be given or awarded. Most of his purchases now were at once rash and comforting, expensive smoked salmon, a Melton Mowbray pie, a bar of milk chocolate, double cream and a bottle of sparkling wine. He also bought bacon, celery, tomatoes, bananas, bread and washing-up liquid. He held and carried his bags home awkwardly because of his stick and slowly because he knew the evil hour, which he had been putting off, was about to catch up with him.

In The Nest he dumped his bags on the kitchen table, divested himself of his outer garments, entered his front room, scene of his efforts to reconcile the religions of mankind, and collapsed in the armchair against the wall.

He could not work. He could not concentrate or face it. He shook. He shook inwardly although he could hold his head steady. His heart was out of control – he would have to get the pills prescribed by Scram, and swallow them even if they proved to be as poisonous as the other pills he had tried to take. His book was not entirely to blame, but it was helping to shorten his life. He sat in the chair with his eyes closed, and his mind veered protectively into unliterary areas. He thought of his love life or lack thereof. It was ancient history rather than present pain.

Puberty hit him late and amidships. What manhood meant to him was responsibility – sooner or later he was going to be under pressure to do something to somebody that he had no inclination to do. He was scared of girls. He only knew one, Zinnia, who was girl enough to render celibacy an attractive option. He was more at ease with men, but anemone-like when he entertained the notion of homosexuality. In his mid-twenties he was bullied by Max to invest in a prostitute. 'Fiasco' would be too weak a word to describe his experience. He never looked at the potential pillager of his virginity. In her room with the gas fire and the sleeping cat he was embarrassingly premature. The money he paid went down the drain, and, back at home with his mother, he committed himself to bachelordom, to study, religion, and the existence of a secular monk.

At that point his train of thought crashed into Zinnia's ice cream, possibly rippling with her blood. In St Columb's he had made a blasphemous connection between the blood of Zinnia and symbolically the blood of the Saviour. He had gone farther, and linked that connection with his lifelong subconscious distaste for the blood that plays its part in Christian worship. In his chair, as armchair critic, he dared to wonder if all religions stained by blood were at fault and out of date, to put it mildly.

But – and this was where things became personal – he had dedicated his life to writing a justification of religion in general, explaining why it was essential to the human race, celebrating the beauty of its submissiveness to higher authority, its altruism, the glory of its martyrs and saints, the reassurance of its message and the consolation of its rites. Was it all a sham? His book was meant to express an argument and an opinion with which he was not sure that he agreed. It could be waste paper. Did it deserve to be finished at long last?

Here was another disturbing question: why was God presiding over the possible destruction of an honest effort to glorify every aspect of His power?

Again, how could He stoop to make the miserable life of His glorifier many times more miserable?

God had created logic, and logic was 'walloping'

the breath of life out of Robin's faith. Religion always was and would be a tense relationship between logic and faith, and logic was coming out on top. He had often stumbled over the block of transubstantiation – in straightforward terms, Christianity claimed that it could convert wine into blood, the blood of Jesus and a memorial of His existence and teaching, but the wine was plonk, the blood of Jesus would be two thousand years old, and to drink blood was a form of cannibalism. Also, into the bargain, to drink it was to align the thousand million Christians worldwide with mosquitoes and vampire bats.

Robin Antrobus sat in his front room, trembling. His train of thought had taken him to the gates of hell. He had crossed frontiers and barriers with foolhardy abandon. It must stop, he must stop, otherwise... The otherwise frightened him so much that he stood up, feeling as if he were waking from a nightmare, and scuttled into the kitchen.

He resolved to eat the Melton Mowbray pie. A chunk of meat and pastry might bring him down to earth. Besides, the time was one o'clock, lunchtime, and he required nourishment if he was not to die of either terror, malnutrition or one of his other ailments.

He unpacked the pie, set the kitchen table, and sat down. Then it occurred to him that he was being contrary, prolonging his life or trying to, while wishing he was dead.

He forced himself to finish his pie, and managed a banana and a cup of tea: he was too tired to act on the argument that he should starve himself. Tradition and habit came to the rescue. He was comforted by milk chocolate. He returned to the armchair in the front room. The whirl of pros and cons in his head was suddenly soporific – nature insisted on a respite.

He awoke to a recurrence of his unprecedented doubts. He was persuaded that something really bad was going to happen, probably to him, possibly to the wider world. He should seek advice, issue a warning. He would have loved to talk to Zinnia; but she would not be pleased to know that, metaphorically, it was her blood that he had slipped up on. Besides, she was at work with those hard-headed lawyers – she would have no time for his forebodings.

What about Max? At least he was unlikely to be busy. But Max would rejoice to see how low the mighty or mightier had fallen. He would put his foot on the neck of Robin as he lay in the dust and ashes of his scholarship and money.

Of course he should go to Hubert Greenstock, who personified Christianity in action. Hubert ought to know how to help a sinner suffering a crisis of conscience. Again there were difficulties. He would want to know why, at Holy Communion, Robin had walked out of St Columb's just before he delivered his words of wisdom. He would not be above airing a grievance.

Robin realised that he had no one to call upon in his hour of need. His shyness had rationalised his withdrawn way of living. He simply could not pretend to be hail-fellow-well-met. Peace and quiet, or as much of them as his neighbours allowed, were the prerequisites of his love of God and his labour of love. Only his mother had been his true companion and helpmeet. During her life he had not looked for companionship elsewhere, it would have complicated matters, and after her death he was unwilling to change anything that he and she had found satisfactory and enjoyable.

Panic seemed to spread like toxic gas through his formerly salubrious home. He could not wait within its four walls to be suffocated and poisoned. He made a bee-line for his British Warm and pork-pie hat. He seized his stick although he was indifferent to muggers and murderers. He opened his front door and slammed it shut behind him.

The weather was not bad for the moment. The sun shone, notwithstanding the grey humidity of earlier in the day, and was welcome even if its rays had that febrile brightness of the winter months. Robin walked towards Roebuck Buildings, skirted it by taking a turning to the left, followed the road called Roebuck Villas and ended in the Rec, often spelt Wreck, the Roebuck Recreation Ground.

Part of the Rec was like a park, an expanse of grass dotted about with leafless trees, part was football and cricket pitches, and part was tennis and basketball courts. Robin walked along the asphalt path to a certain seat, on which he had often rested. He was relieved to see nobody sitting on it, and sat in the middle so as to leave little room for an outsider to join him. Toddlers with their mothers passed by, and younger children sleeping in push-chairs. Little girls chased one another in the middle distance and little boys kicked balls and quarrelled. Farther off, school games were being played and shouts mingled with the whistles of referees.

A strain of wistfulness forced an entry into Robin's desperation. Should he have tried harder to become a family man? But he could not have coped with marital rights, and a wife and offspring would have played havoc with his routine.

The weather changed: nature seemed to mirror his glum mood. The sun was obscured, black clouds tinged with lurid orange raced across the sky – they were mysterious, he had not noticed them before. Darkness descended on the Rec, and unexpectedly, before Robin had adjusted to the omens above, a dazzling fork of lightning speared or appeared to spear into the ground close by his seat. He stood up, full of involuntary fear – again contrarily, to be struck by lightning would solve all his problems. Thunder crashed and rolled – the storm was over his head. He thought of shelter, but where? He raised his eyes, pleadingly perhaps, and saw the clouds part and heard a voice, a deep bass enormously powerful voice, saying: 'You are the crown prince of my kingdom.'

5

The shock caused something like temporary concussion. He was aware of being rained on, of sitting on the tarmac path with his legs under him and huge drops of rain falling on his bare head.

Where was his pork-pie? He looked round apprehensively, not for his missing headgear but to see if he could be seen, sitting in a heap on the ground. Then he thought: how can I be so petty? How can I worry about an old hat and my dignity after what has happened to me?

He stayed put. He did not try to stand up, or care if strangers disapproved of him. He was preoccupied. What had happened? He scrupled to put a name to the event. He believed or imagined that he had heard a voice, a loud voice, speaking to him personally from high in the sky. And it had said, or seemed to say, something so strange, so extraordinary, so flattering and compli-mentary, that he blushed to remember or perhaps to dream it.

The rain pelted down on him and he took no notice. He believed he had heard the voice of God. And God had told him that he was in line for a position and an honour beyond human hierarchical cognisance.

It could not be true. The voice had resembled that of the father of Bambi in the Walt Disney film. Bambi loses his mother, the deer, and an unseen agent, maybe the stag, informs him in reverberating tones that 'Man has taken her away' – meaning, although children did not know it, that she had been killed and eaten. Robin said to himself: 'Ridiculous!' He suspected foul play, that someone had played a practical joke on him with a megaphone or a loudhailer. He looked round, but his view was obscured by the rain, and so far as he could make out he was alone in the Rec. Could the voice have come from a nearby dwelling? But no dwellings were close enough; and on second thoughts he was certain – certain rightly or wrongly – that he had been addressed from on high.

He shook himself mentally. He was perturbed by his involuntary recourse to religious phraseology. Surely it was not God who had addressed Bambi. And surely God had not stooped to speak to him, let alone to say he had been picked to be second in command of the heavenly hosts. No – he had to stop thinking along those lines and in those terms, he had to pull himself together, for he was already soaked to the skin and needed and wanted to get home as soon as possible. He began to struggle to his feet – he was still weak at the knees, and his hand slipped when he grasped the wet metal of the seat.

'Good afternoon, Mr Antrobus.'

'What?'

He had jumped to the conclusion that God

was expressing an afterthought; but it was a female voice this time, and it issued from a youngish woman under an umbrella.

He recognised her, he knew her slightly. She was the daughter of the Patels, Jayendra and Sanjana, the newsagents. She was plain and had been a trouble to her parents.

'Oh,' he said. 'Good afternoon.'

'Can I help you, Mr Antrobus? You're wet through.'

'Oh, thank you, no – I'm on my way home and was caught in the storm.'

'Have you a brolly?'

'No, but I do have a hat somewhere.'

He was now on his feet, and he spotted the pork-pie, bent and picked it up, and water poured out of it.

'Oh dear,' he said.

'Please share my brolly, Mr Antrobus, sir – I'll be passing your house, I'm going to call on my Mum and Dad.'

'Oh well, thank you, you're very kind.'

He gave in; but was in no mood for company.

They walked towards Roebuck Road through the rain. She commented on the weather. He tried to remember her name.

At length he said: 'Aren't you Indira?'

'Used to be,' she replied. She spoke good English, but it still sounded Indian.

'I know – you called yourself Indy – isn't that right?'

'Not by quite a chalk. I never liked the name they gave me, but I was displeased when it was

63

shortened at school. "Indy" equals indigestion. Now I've changed my name.'

'Are you married?'

'No fear! I changed my first name and my second. I wanted to be an Englishwoman.'

'What is it?'

'Wendy Paddle.'

He would have seen the funny side of the transformation of Indira Patel into Wendy Paddle if he had not had such a weight on his mind.

He sloshed along, vaguely conscious of the wetness of his shoes. Near Roebuck Buildings he imagined Max's response to his experience, and it caused him to stumble.

'Is something wrong, sir?' Wendy inquired.

'No,' he fibbed.

After a slight pause he added: 'Not really – no – not at all.'

They walked in silence almost to the door of 7 Roebuck Road.

He stopped and turned towards her. She had granny glasses halfway down her nose.

'Are you religious?' he asked.

She stared at him, then answered rather as if he had made an improper suggestion: 'Oh Mr Antrobus!'

'I'm sorry, I just wondered,' he told her. 'Thank you again. Goodbye.' And he hurried up his garden path and let himself into the sanctuary of home as quickly as he could.

He let his sodden British Warm fall on to the tiled floor of the hall, hung his hat on a doorknob, kicked off his shoes, and squelched in his wet socks up to his bathroom, undressed, donned his dressing-gown, and in his bedroom clambered into the unmade bed and pulled the covers up to his chin.

His moment of exaltation, when he had felt able to assure Wendy Paddle that nothing was wrong, had passed. He was chilled to the bone and would probably catch cold. He was always ill if he had been out in the rain. He must have made a mistake about that voice through the clouds. To receive messages from nowhere was notoriously pathological. Was he round the bend? If so, where would he end up?

Gradually his circulation changed the colours of his reasoning. The head-cold in store for him would have been caught in a good cause. To be ill was less important than to be blessed. He was not 'mental' – he had been sane enough for too long to be suddenly insane – and was a bit young for senile dementia. He had definitely heard a voice, and received its message loud and clear. He had been informed confidentially that he was singled out for preferment in the next world.

Of course he had to die in order to come into his inheritance. He had been considering suicide when the powers-that-be – he skirted round more particular designations – revealed their plan to reward him in the afterlife. Could it be not that he had been offered encouragement to carry on living, but presented with another argument in favour of *felo de se*?

He shied away from such a gloomy deduction.

He side-stepped the deeper analyses of the episode in the Rec. His work in progress might be *The Analogical Review of Religions*, a work of exhaustive historical criticism, but his brain refused to review the topic of the day, he was somehow unable as well as unwilling to criticise eight little words. He was the recipient of an extraordinary message. Without false modesty, he had to admit that he seemed to be the subject of a miracle, destined for a seat next to the Ruler of the Universe, and, by implication, even to have prospects beyond such a distinction. Incredible or not, glory suffused his battered old being like a heat-rash. How happy his mother would have been to know that he had made better than good after all, and how surprised she would be one day if there was any truth in the doctrine of resurrection! And what a snub to his father!

He gloated, his recollections and expectations became entangled, a mixture of shock and his exposure to the weather had their effects, and he either slept or lost full consciousness.

He was woken or recalled from elsewhere by the telephone. His bedroom was dark, and his heart hammered apprehensively – he was seldom rung up, he always feared the worst when he was rung, and why was he in bed?

He rushed downstairs in his bare feet with his dressing-gown flapping. He thought: I must not fall and break my bones. Remembrance was like rebirth. He remembered everything and felt equal to life for a change. He lifted the receiver.

'Are you all right?' Max asked.

'Oh, it's you,' he said.

'Nothing wrong?'

'You're the second person who's asked me today. No – the opposite.'

'What's that?'

'What time is it?'

'Six o'clock. You're not ill, are you?'

'Why do you think I am?'

'Well, not knowing the time – and blowing like a grampus – and I saw you in the road in the storm this afternoon.'

'Oh – that.'

'You were with a woman. I could see you from my windows.'

'That doesn't mean I was ill or am ill.'

'Very well. Goodbye.'

'Max!'

'Yes?'

'It's a long story.'

'What is?'

'Could you have dinner with me?'

'This evening?'

'Yes.'

'It's not Sunday, you know.'

'I do know.'

'Let me look in my diary.'

'Oh Max!' Robin scolded – he was exasperated by the charade – Max seldom had any engagements written in his diary – and would have known if he was about to be involved in a social gathering.

'All clear,' Max said. 'You're pushing the boat out, aren't you – two dinners to pay for in one week?'

'Money's beside the point.'

'Is it, by Jove! I'll be along in an hour.'

Robin did not regret his invitation, as he might have done yesterday. A new decisiveness stirred within him: he was no longer in a hurry to kill himself, whether or not someone up there had extended a sort of welcome. He washed and dressed, and resolved to invest in clothes more suited to present circumstances. He also prepared for an especially bruising session with Max, who considered that his God was superior to Robin's, and was bound to be resentful that Robin had already stolen a march on him in the ultimate country.

While he waited for his cousin, and after he had put his wet clothes to dry in the kitchen, he peeped into his workroom. He had been curious. How would he now react to the scene of his failure? He was not upset. The piled papers, evidence of his application or misapplication, struck him as out of date. Yet those laborious years were not wasted, he was certain of it, for his religionism if not his religion, his lifelong interest in religion, was connected somehow with that offer of the happiest and most wonderful of endings.

He opened his front door to Max.

Robin had donned a raincoat and a trilby that had belonged to his father. Max commented on the change of attire. Robin explained that his British Warm and cap were still wet. Max seemed to be dissatisfied by this answer. He was encased in his ankle-length Australian overcoat, as usual.

'It's stopped raining,' Robin observed.

'Not for long,' Max returned.

They walked side by side along Roebuck Road in the direction of Ab's Caf, Robin on tiptoe in a metaphorical sense, Max heavy-footed.

'What's this about?' Max asked.

'I'll tell you when we get there,' Robin replied.

'Nothing bad?'

'No.'

They reached the restaurant. It was nearly empty, and Mirrie was hen-pecking Ab in the kitchen, while Debra looked droopy behind the counter.

Ab emerged and greeted them.

'Good evening, gentlemen – nice to see you on a weekday – is it a celebration?'

'Yes and no,' Robin said, and Max shrugged his shoulders as he clambered out of his coat.

They were seated at their usual table and ordered their escalopes. Then Robin ordered a bottle of a low-priced Italian wine with bubbles in it.

'What's the wine in aid of?' Max demanded as soon as they were alone.

'You remember this afternoon's storm?' Robin began.

'What's wine got to do with it?'

'Well, I was in the Rec, I was sitting there and not feeling too good.'

'Ill, you mean?'

'Sort of – sick of everything – you know.'

'I'm not sure I do.'

'Anyway, there was a big clap of thunder – I'm not sure about the lightning.'

'Were you unconscious?'

69

'Certainly not. I must have been absent-minded. I think there was lightning. Anyway, the thunder was very loud and seemed to be immediately overhead. Then I heard a voice.'

'Sorry?'

'I heard a voice.'

'Whose voice?'

'That's the whole point.'

'I will say you've taken your time to get to the point. Go on! You heard a voice?'

'It was very loud, deafening almost, and I believe it was addressing me.'

'What was it saying and who did it belong to?'

'I can't answer your second question beyond the shadow of doubt.'

'Well – answer the first.'

'That's difficult. I'd rather have a shot at the second.'

'Okay – I'm waiting.'

'God.'

'I beg your pardon?'

'In my considered opinion it was the voice of God.'

'Are you teasing me, Robin?'

'No.'

'Are you feeling better now?'

'Yes.'

'So you heard the voice of the Almighty?'

'Don't sneer at me, Max.'

'What did He have to tell you?'

'You'll only laugh.'

'I won't. I'm serious. What did you hear? What were the words you heard?'

70

'I'm embarrassed to repeat them.'

'Be brave!'

' "You are the crown prince of my Kingdom".'

Max flushed as if with some strong emotion, anger or at least irritation or perhaps scepticism, said nothing, but after a moment moved convulsively, kicking out a leg that connected with a leg of the table, and simultaneously slapping his forehead with his hand.

Ab arrived with the wine, showing the bottle, and spouting sales talk.

'Please open it,' Robin said.

Max chimed in, 'I need a drink badly.'

'And pour it out,' Robin instructed Ab.

Max snatched his full glass, drank the contents, held it out for Robin to refill, and said: 'I'm afraid you're a lot sicker than you thought you were. See Scram without delay, that's my advice.'

'No, Max – calm down – I'm well, better than I've been, as a matter of fact – and I asked you out to dinner so that we could discuss the occurrence in a rational manner.'

'Rational? I'm rational. I can't say that I think you are.'

'It's no good huffing and puffing. You're a religious man. You should take an interest in what may be an event of considerable religious significance. Don't just brush it aside. Here's our food now.'

Debra placed full plates before them and mouthed a 'There you go' together with a simpering smile.

'What is there to discuss?' Max asked, loading his fork.

'Can you believe my story?'

'I cannot.'

'In that case, will you explain what happened?'

'You dreamed it.'

'No – I was on my feet at the relevant time – I had risen to my feet because I was alarmed by the thunder.'

'Well, you hallucinated.'

'No – I've never experienced an hallucination – and I promise you I wasn't unwell in the Rec – and feel okay now.'

'Were other people around? Could some yob have been responsible?'

'A yob with knowledge of the Book of Common Prayer?'

'What type of voice was it?'

'Bass.'

'Oxford accent?'

'Yes.'

'He sounded English?'

'Yes.'

'An English gentleman?'

'Approximately.'

'Yes – well – I suppose we can't be sure God's a gentleman, or that he's English. Do you know anybody with a voice like that?'

'Maybe.'

'Who?'

'Bambi's father.'

Robin giggled and Max could not help joining in. Max prolonged the humorous interval by

confessing that he had been about to exclaim:
'Good God!'

They munched their food, then Max resumed
his interrogation.

'Have you seen the Bambi film lately?'

'No.'

'Repeat the sentence you heard!'

Robin did so.

'It's funny,' Max said.

'I agree, but how particularly funny do you
mean?'

'We've heard of the King of Heaven, but the
Crown Prince is hard to swallow.'

'Talking about the Crown Prince isn't much
odder than talking to me in a thunderstorm.'

'Granted – but where does Jesus fit in? If
heaven's a monarchy, the Son of God would be
Crown Prince. And Jesus told us that He was
the Son of God. How do you explain that?'

'I can't explain anything, Max. I didn't ask
you out to dinner in order to explain. I'm
mystified, and I hoped we might arrive at an
explanation by putting our heads together.'

'Well – frankly, Robin, I'm bowled over, and
not only by the idea, also by your taking the
idea seriously, that you're damn near a god already
and in line for the top job. I'm not trying to
be funny when I say that God alone knows how
you can presume to fancy you're capable and
worthy. You're not even a Catholic.'

They were interrupted. Debra collected their
plates, and Ab came over and took orders for
Max's Peach Melba and Robin's vanilla ice.

'I presume nothing,' Robin said, 'but it's quite nice that somebody thinks well of me – you must see that.'

'Thinking well of you isn't the same as telling you you're going to be the Almighty.'

'You're twisting everything. You are!'

'Am I? If you say so, you'd better turn me into a pillar of salt.'

'Don't be silly. I guessed you'd be jealous, Max.'

'Jealous, nothing! I've never been jealous of you. It's more the other way round.'

'Don't let's quarrel.'

'Who's quarrelling?'

Max drank the last drops of the wine in his glass, and looked round at the bar, perhaps in hopes of prompting Ab to suggest another bottle. But Ab was back in the kitchen with Mirrie – he had a weakness for persecution; and Robin was loath to increase his cousin's intake of alcohol and cantankerousness.

Debra served the ices, glumly muttering, 'Enjoy!'

Max reopened the conversation.

'Who was the woman with you under the umbrella?'

'She doesn't count.'

'Do I know her?'

'Probably. Her name's Wendy Paddle.'

'Wendy what?'

'Paddle. She's the Patel's daughter. She's changed her name from Indira Patel.'

'She hasn't done herself a favour. Wendy Paddle

74

– it's more alien than Indira Patel. I remember her, a girl with eyebrows and glasses. Is she a friend of yours?'

'Acquaintance. She took pity on me in the Rec, when I'd heard the voice and was lying on the ground, getting wetter.'

'Why were you on the ground? Had you suffered a seizure or something?'

'No, Max. I'd slipped and fallen. I have not had a seizure or a stroke.'

'Did Wendy Paddle hear the voice?'

'I don't know, she didn't mention it. I asked her if she was religious while I was sheltering under her umbrella, and she seemed to regard my question as a proposition.'

'Does she attract you?'

'No, not in the slightest.'

'She's a lapsed Muslim, she won't go to the Mosque with her parents.'

'Really? What am I to do, Max?'

'That's an awkward question.'

'Exactly. I could do nothing, or I could go public.'

'Or pick Zinnia's brains.'

'Zinnia makes my blood run cold.'

'That's her speciality.'

'Can I face Zinnia?'

'I'll have to tell her, Robin. I let on that I was having dinner with you, and she wanted to know why, why midweek instead of on Sunday.'

'Oh God!'

'God ought to protect you – you're more a member of His family now than of ours.'

Robin had to laugh this time. The cousins joined in somewhat conspiratorial laughter, as if nervous of being overheard by the person in question.

The meal was finished. Robin paid the bill and the cousins walked homewards.

'Have you had the results of your tests? I'm sorry I didn't ask you before,' Robin said.

'No problem to speak of,' Max replied.

'I'm glad. And how's the company doctor doing?'

'Business is slow at present.'

'It may pick up.'

'I'd be grateful for a miracle, Robin.'

6

That night, or in the early morning of the next day, Robin awoke to a feeling of rapture. He was the poor in spirit who had been blessed. He had been raised up, lifted from a bottomless pit to a dizzying height. His heart beat with renewed force and regularity. His temple throbbed, and his throat contracted owing to a lump not of sorrow but joy.

It was temporary. Everything subsided; and, although he had never in his whole life felt quite so happy, he remembered his mother's warnings that over-excitement was bound to end in tears or illness.

He refused to be cast down. He swapped his usual prayer, 'Thy will be done', for 'Alleluia'. He had no symptoms of ill-health despite his soaking, his stressful meeting with Max, and the unprecedented excitation. He had every reason to think of himself as a new man, and therefore the advice of his mother might not apply.

He had slept enough. He got up and began his day. Every sound was rendered tuneful in his ears. The roars and clangs of the refuse lorry were a celebration of life. Ben the milkman's electric float was musical, and the footfalls of the business people scurrying to and fro were poetic. Bill Rickitt's morning rigmarole and a swearword chorus between himself and Marge, and then the noisiness of Kylie and Clay, did not annoy him; while the bumps and twitters of Rhoda and Ruth on the other side of The Nest were almost soothing.

Robin had an appetite for his muesli, and dared to have a cup of Nescafé instead of tea. Work, the old routine, he relegated to the future. He also managed not to be bothered by Max's destructive tendencies. He decided to walk out and buy a newspaper: he thought a change would be as good as a holiday.

He wore his raincoat again, although it was not raining: the British Warm was still damp. The weather was grey, but neither windy nor cold. He breathed in the metropolitan form of ozone, the smells of life, food, carbon dioxide and internal combustion, with satisfaction. Jayendra Patel was behind the counter in his shop and they exchanged greetings. Robin looked at *The Times*, then in his devil-may-care mood picked a lurid tabloid.

'All well, Mr Antrobus?' Jayendra asked. He was big and friendly and polite.

'Yes, thanks. Your daughter did me a good turn yesterday.'

'I'm glad to hear there's something good about her.'

'She let me take refuge under her umbrella.'

'She told us. She was a little concerned. But you look well, if I may say it.'

'I'm okay, thank you, and please thank Wendy again.'

'Wendy, who is she? Our daughter is Indira Patel. We don't know any Wendy Paddles who live in Kilburn and work in beauty parlours, which are indecent.'

'I'm sorry, Jayendra.'

'She's a blasphemer, Mr Antrobus.'

'A nice one, though.'

'It's not nice to break our hearts.'

'I'm sure she'll win you round. She's a modern miss, that's all.'

'All too much, Mr Antrobus, when we love her so.'

Other people came into the shop and Robin returned to The Nest.

His telephone was ringing.

He lifted the receiver and Zinnia said: 'What do you think you're doing, Robin?' – with a strong emphasis on the 'do'.

'I've been to buy a newspaper,' he retorted.

'You know perfectly well what I mean. You can't start hearing voices. I'm horrified and so is Max. I want to talk to you without delay. Let's have lunch together. I'll call for you at one o'clock sharp.'

'Zinnia, stop bullying, please.'

'Bullying? I'm not bullying, I'm trying to stop you making a complete fool of yourself. Are you free for lunch?'

'Today? Won't you be at the office?'

'I've taken time off to sort you out. If you can't have lunch, I'll come round now and give you a piece of my mind.'

'Make it lunch, Zinnia – but I won't be scolded
– you won't find me here unless you promise to
behave decently.'

'Oh very well.'

She rang off.

Robin's only telephone was located in the
hallway of The Nest. His father had installed it
there many years ago, and he had never thought
of moving it. The instrument sat on an occasional
table beside a wooden-seated chair. He subsided
on to the chair.

Weakness had replaced vigour. He had always
hated to be or be thought to be in the wrong.
He was a goody-goody. Zinnia was either a thorn
in his flesh or a blow on his head by a blunt
instrument: those were the metaphors that
described their relationship. She had ordered him
about on the beaches of their summer holidays,
and knocked flat his sand castles which were
prettier than hers; and now she had fired a
broadside at his castle in the air.

Zinnia exemplified the proposition that a coarse
woman is coarser than a coarse man. Her lavatorial
jokes when they were children had been disgusting.
Her obsession with sex even at her present age
was repellent. The fear she inspired in men had
not been the sort that forced them towards
marriage. She was becoming one of those phallic
spinsters who bellow their challenges at possible
partners. Robin feared that, for her, in a sexual
context, he sometimes looked better than nothing.
He submitted to the strain and stress of their
meetings nonetheless, he was charitable and

favoured the easy option. But today, this morning, because of who he had been told he was and would be, he had stood up to her. The trouble was that his defiance on the telephone exhausted his store of energy.

He went into his workroom and collapsed in the big armchair. It resembled the womb. He closed his eyes and shut out the world. Time passed. He might have slept. Drowsily, he prayed for the strength to forgive those who trespassed against him. He would postpone work, and postponement could be more permanent than temporary. He could see that the title of his book, arrived at by much cogitation, *The Analogical Review of Religions*, was a yawn. It was worse, esoteric verging on meaningless.

His doorbell rang.

He was unready for it. He jumped to his feet, wondering how he could have let the morning slip by and why his heart seemed to be in his mouth. He rushed to open the door and wished he had put Zinnia in her place by making her wait.

Max was there, too.

Robin said: 'I wasn't expecting you.'

Zinnia said: 'It's family business,' and extended her neck so that her cheek could be pecked.

Max said: 'We'll pay our whack, don't worry.'

Robin left them standing in the porch. His British Warm was dry and he had to get into it. Mistakes and misunderstandings were already the order of the day.

He returned in a conciliatory mood.

'I'm glad you're joining us, Max. Will Ab's Caf do, Zinnia – my treat?' he inquired. He had reflected that he would be more at their mercy if he was their guest.

Zinnia was gracious, Max managed a mumble, and they walked along Roebuck Road, commenting on the weather.

Ab's greeting was excessive, and to honour Zinnia he summoned Mirrie, whose fleshiness and blood-red cheeks were no doubt why she found fault with her weedy spouse. He also insisted on presenting them with aperitifs, sweet wine in very small glasses. The three cousins were seated where the two usually sat, and they ordered their meal – Max and Robin wanted escalopes and Zinnia said impatiently that the same would do.

But Zinnia had a little something to add to these preliminaries. She levelled an accusation at her cousin and brother. She laughed at them for eating the same meal for years without number.

'You're Blimps,' she said. 'You're dodos, and fit to be extinct.'

The dodos smirked uneasily.

'Now, Robin,' Zinnia rapped out, 'I'd like to hear your side of the story.'

He obliged, he had been prepared to do so, but he cut his account to the bone.

'Is that all?' she demanded.

'What more could there be?' he countered.

'You mean it was God Himself who spoke to you?'

'I mean to tell the truth.'

'But you think it was God?'

'I'm trying to think who else it might have been.'

'It could well have been a professional magician – conjurors say they're illusionists nowadays. I think you've been tricked.'

'Do you have any more proof that it was a trickster than I have that the voice was supernatural?'

'I've more common sense than you and common sense proves it. You've always had your head in the clouds, and now you fancy someone in the sky spoke to you and you alone. It's unbelievable, and what was said is unbelievable. God can't be a king in the sense of the word "king". He wouldn't have the equivalent of a Prince of Wales. We're Christians and Christians have faith that Jesus was His son. You'd be sacrilegious if you weren't being silly, Robin. Why on earth would God want you to have a managerial role in the kingdom of heaven? And was He hinting that you were due to take over from Him?'

Max put his oar in.

'Funny if you were God-in-waiting, Robin – a bit of a leg-up.'

Zinnia weighed in again.

'You must see it's funny, Robin. You of all people! I thought that as a family we knew our station in life. We were never presumptuous people, even if your mother was a snob and tried to look down on us. And you've always been a particularly modest person, puddling along with your books and never getting anywhere. Now in your dotage you tell us you're going to be God.'

'I told no one that.'

'What you've told us amounts to that. Your mother spoilt you. I suppose she gave you the idea that you were so important. Well, I'm sorry to have to say it, Robin, but you're not my idea of the Almighty, and I can't see my friends getting down on their knees to pray to you for their daily bread.'

All three of them giggled at her belligerence. It was also amusing that she mentioned bread just as Ab and Debra served their food. Another bottle of Ab's fizzy wine was served, and the cousins' conversation resumed in between intervals of eating and drinking.

'Anyway,' Zinnia said, 'what's to be done, Robin?'

'What?'

'You'll have to do something. You can't be passive in this instance as you have been in so many others.'

'I have no plans, I'm not an activist or a militant, like you.'

'Too true! But I can't stand idly by while you lose your head.'

'I'm not losing my head, I'm sane, and not short of common sense. I've had a very strange experience, but there are more things in heaven and earth than even you know, Zinnia. I informed Max, I felt I had to, and I'm beginning to regret it. To answer your question, I'm doing nothing whatsoever.'

Max said to Zinnia: 'I advised him to see Scram, who'd give him pills.'

'Scram's useless,' she retorted. 'He needs a shrink.' She addressed Robin more directly. 'You must know that hearing voices is a symptom of the early stage of dementia. We'd like to get you to a doctor who specialises in mental health.'

'Don't be stupid, Zinnia.'

'I'm afraid you're the stupid one to call me stupid, Robin. You're not with it. You're out to lunch in every sense of the words. The phrase "not all there" fits you like a glove. Let me remind you that I've had more success in my life than you and my brother put together. I wear the trousers in fact – I'm wearing them right now – and figuratively. It's no mistake that I'm sitting between you, at the top of this table, where the head of the family sits, and insisting that you must receive the right sort of medical help.'

'Well, Zinnia, listen to me! I'm snapping my fingers at you. Do you hear? And please stop your beastly bullying.'

'I won't be called beastly, Robin, not after I've given up a whole day's pay to help you.'

'You weren't asked for help, and so far neither of you have said anything helpful.'

'You're most ungrateful.'

'Shut up, Zinnia! You're eating at my expense. I've let you be offensive. I'm not the ungrateful one.'

Zinnia blushed, for once she seemed to be at a disadvantage, and Max interrupted a pregnant pause.

'Steady on, you two,' he said.

Robin spoke.

'I do have problems of one sort and another, and I wouldn't mind discussing one of them. Here it is. Yesterday at the Rec at round about three o'clock there was a clap of thunder – I remember lightning too – and a very loud voice through storm clouds spoke to me. Rain then fell, I was caught in a deluge, and the Patels' daughter came along and shared her umbrella with me all the way back to The Nest. To the best of my knowledge the Rec had been empty at the relevant time. Who spoke the words I distinctly heard, who were they addressed to, and what did they mean? Serious answers to those questions would be welcome.'

Zinnia spoke.

'My answers are that it wasn't God, and you weren't being spoken to by anybody, and the sentence you think you heard is tommy-rot.'

'I said "serious", Zinnia.'

Max cleared his throat.

'Here's my opinion. The voice was jiggery-pokery – some artful monkey "threw" it into the sky – high-tech stuff. The message wasn't for Robin, it was aimed at another party, and the wording was ever so slightly different. I'm saying the sentence ran, "You are the crown princess of my kingdom", and the person who should have got it was Wendy Paddle.'

Robin and Zinnia laughed in unison.

Robin exclaimed, 'Crippen,' and Zinnia asked 'She's the Patels' girl – is a Patel to be God now?'

Max explained: 'Wendy was in the wrong place at the right time, so she missed her message and Robin got it instead. Wendy's a bright girl, and she's being courted by a Muslim boy she doesn't take to. Wendy's boyfriend wants her to help run his kingdom, which probably amounts to a shop. You may laugh at me, but I've made more sense of yesterday's mystery than anyone else. And I've corroboration, which is more than you have.'

'Corroboration?' the others chorused.

Max supplied it.

'Nobody in Roebuck Buildings heard the message, although some of the people on the Rec side of the building did hear thunder. I've also had a word with Jayendra Patel. His choice of a husband for Wendy – Indira, as he still calls her – is an electronic engineer whose parents live in a house on the far side of the Recreation Ground.'

Zinnia began to say, 'It's not convincing...' when Robin interrupted to ask: 'Have you discussed my situation with all and sundry, Max?'

'Well, it's not a secret, is it?'

'Of course it is. Where do you think your gossiping leaves me? Every inhabitant of London, of England or the whole world, will think I'm either God or crazy.'

'Hold your horses, Robin!'

'Zinnia, please deal with your brother.'

She said: 'Who have you talked to, Max?'

'No one apart from the ones mentioned, and I had a word with Father Murphy.'

Ab and Debra approached to remove plates, and predictable Peach Melbas were ordered for the two Joneses – Robin refused the offer of an ice.

As soon as they were alone he declaimed in an almost tearful voice: 'Why did I ever confide in you, Max? Why did I trust you?'

'Cheer up, old boy – I've done you a favour when you think of it – you may be able to cash in whatever the rights and wrongs are.'

'Oh Max,' Robin reproached him.

Zinnia said: 'Let's agree to keep our counsel and do some pondering.'

'But Max has thrown me to the wolves. The last thing I wanted was to have the Roman Catholics at my throat. I won't be exploited, and I won't exploit myself. I'm not a crown prince of anywhere, and I refuse to play god. My work's gone haywire, my life likewise – and my life's under threat. Everything's topsy-turvy, and I don't know what to do or what to expect.'

Zinnia said: 'There, there! You needn't get so excited. Don't forget the possibility that you really may have been singled out by heaven for a reward beyond our comprehension. Max, be careful! We'd be wise not to incur Robin's wrath. I'm not joking. Scepticism is all very well, but he is entitled to a little more than our respect and affection – we haven't heard a voice from nowhere. Thank you for feeding us, Robin.'

She added satirically: 'Max, put your thinking cap on.'

7

That afternoon Robin was unwell. There was no doubt about it. Sitting in the armchair in his workroom he somehow boiled over – he was bubbling with heat and overflowing with sweat. It was not hypochondria. It was nothing like Max's illnesses, which never tested positive.

He was not sure how long it lasted. He did cool down in the end. Unfortunately his heart then fluttered into the scene. He could not suppress a twinge of amusement: his heart was like a fledgling flapping its wings in The Nest. But the flutters were not funny, they were frightening. He kept on thinking they would stop either at the top of their rise or the bottom of their fall.

Again in the end the beating of his heart stabilised. The time was four-thirty. He was able to go into the kitchen and drink a glass of water. He tried not to be cross with himself, for he knew he should have kept his temper at Ab's Caf – his cousins had been maddening, but he should have risen above their typical teasing. He, or they, or the three of them had caused what was suspiciously like a heart attack. He must curb his emotions, he must practise self-control.

He longed to be in the horizontal, and mounted the stairs slowly. He lay on his bed and again slipped into recuperative slumber.

He awoke. He felt better. Night had fallen. It was six forty-five. He considered his options.

He could seek medical assistance via Scram. He should definitely do so for his heart's sake; and, in his cousins' opinions, his brain was in need of examination. But he shrank from a shrink, he was convinced that he was saner than the majority of psychiatrists. And he had been ill off and on ever since he was born, and his experience suggested that medical science had proved itself almost as bad for him as good.

There was another reason why he wanted to keep out of Scram's clutches. He would have to reveal that he might be God. Foreseeably, Scram would be inquisitive and snobbish, and broadcast the news that he was patching up at least the heir to the Ruler of the Universe. Scram would be all too keen to write for his patient a prescription unique in medical history. Robin could almost hear him boast: 'I have had the most pukka of all sahibs in my surgery!' He decided not to risk it in the meanwhile: the danger of one or two blips in the cardiac region was preferable to being turned into an Aunt Sally.

The religious question nagged at Robin. His brand of common sense, mocked by his cousins, was well aware of booby-traps ahead. He had already stumbled into one, by sharing his secret with Max, who had passed it on to Father Murphy of all people. Father Murphy was an Irishman from his tonsure to his toes, noted for his indiscretions in the pulpit; and his Irish housekeeper, Mrs Connolly, was a tongue-wagger with a vengeance.

Robin was not a bigot. He prided himself on having approached his writings on religion in a spirit of liberal objectivity. However, more than thirty years of research had not convinced him that priests in general were peace-lovers. He realised that Hubert Greenstock would not be pleased to know that Dylan Murphy was streaking ahead in the race to reach the recipient of the word of God; and that the congregation of St Columb's would be extremely resentful to see that the congregation of St Mary's was winning the prize. There could be trouble not just in store but in holy places. He imagined altercations in church halls and fisticuffs in vestries, and triumphalist and bitter words exchanged under the crucifix. He had to put a spoke in the spinning wheel of events. He must make a moderating move before it was too late.

He revived further with cups of tea as strong as he could swallow. He pondered his course of action until about seven o'clock in the evening, then rang the new St Columb's vicarage, a box-like hideosity built on a site overlooking the graveyard – the Regency vicarage had been sold and was owned and inhabited by two interior decorators, both male.

Dorothea Greenstock answered the telephone. When Robin asked if he was ringing at a bad moment, she said yes, they were having supper, but disappeared before he could say he would try later or else in the morning.

Hubert was audibly masticating as he inquired in an oppressive tone of voice: 'What can I do for you, Robin?'

Robin apologised.

'What is it, Robin?' Hubert asked sharply.

'I'm hoping we could meet.'

'What's it about?'

'It's urgent.'

'How urgent?'

'Hubert, urgent urgent – more urgent would be tautological.'

'I am eating my supper, Robin, and disinclined to discuss syntax.'

'Forgive me – syntax is a red herring – I want to tell you something that I know you'd wish to hear.'

'Please tell me on the telephone.'

'That's impossible. You'd know why if you allowed me to come and talk to you.'

'Oh well – I could probably spare you a few minutes after Matins on Sunday.'

'Sunday! No, Hubert, I'm sorry, it has to be sooner – this evening or early tomorrow. I'm not exaggerating. God's involved.'

'What did you say?'

'Nothing, but believe me, it's urgent all right.'

'I repeat, Robin, that we have not finished our supper. Tomorrow – well, tomorrow, I might be able to fit you in between a funeral and a last rites. There's a ten-minute gap.'

'Ten minutes is better than nothing, but you'll need more time, we both will.'

'I can't keep the last rites waiting.'

'No – very true – all right'

The rest of Robin's evening passed in a swirl of religious elation, irritation with his vicar, uncousinly sentiments, medical dilemmas, and wincing at the noises of his neighbours in their bathroom at bedtime. But he again slept soundly, and wondered in the morning if he had been granted an exceptional version of the peace of God.

His appointment was at ten past ten in the vicarage. Hubert, wearing his dog-collar and ankle-length black and belted cassock, opened his front door with its knocker in the shape of the Christian fish.

He said, looking at his wristwatch, 'I thank you for being punctual. Come into my study, Robin.'

The weather was cold and wooden armchairs stood on either side of an electric fire – two bars, one glowing red – in the small rectangular room with a window at the far end.

'What is it, Robin? I'm afraid we don't have time to beat about the bush.'

'"Beat about the bush" isn't an appropriate metaphor, Hubert.'

'Oh? Are we back on my grammar?'

'Certainly not, far from it. But I can't be rushed.'

'Very well. You said the matter to be discussed was urgent. Is that so?'

'Yes.'

'It's still urgent?'

'Yes.'

'You said something else that has worried me. Am I right in thinking you mentioned God on the telephone yesterday?'

'I did.'

'In what context?'

'He spoke to me.'

'God spoke to you?'

'Exactly – at least that's my belief.'

'It's unlikely – and I could say something more trenchant.'

'Shouldn't you listen to my story before you dismiss it, Hubert?'

'Please continue!'

'I was in the Recreation Ground last Thursday afternoon. It was stormy, there was a clap of thunder, and a deep voice spoke to me.'

'What did it say?'

'"You are the crown prince of my kingdom".'

'Anything else?'

'No. Rain fell and I walked home. I don't believe it was a trick.'

'Were there witnesses?'

'Not that I know of yet. My cousin Max Jones lives in Roebuck Buildings and has tried and failed to find anyone who heard the voice. But the daughter of the Patels, Wendy who was Indira, walked with me to my house – she was in the offing and might have something relevant to say. I'm going to ask her.'

'Robin, Wendy Paddle – the name that Indira

now rejoices in – is neither here nor there. I hasten to add that I speak not as a racist, but from a legal viewpoint. A single source carries very little weight. You are a religious man and a writer. Your interests and your imagination were conceivably the author of the episode. I cast no aspersions on your beliefs, but I'm sure you will soon acknowledge that the Almighty might not take it on Himself to foretell your posthumous future in monarchistic terms which flatly contradict the whole of the New Testament. I hope that, without rushing you, we could leave the matter there.'

'Wait a mo, Hubert.'

'I cannot dally for a reason that you know – Miss Woodly is on her deathbed.'

'What if I'm right and you're wrong?'

Hubert laughed sarcastically.

'I cannot deal with hypotheses.'

'What do you mean? Religion's an hypothesis. But let it pass! I'm not a creative writer or an imaginative man. I am an historian and could cite innumerable mistakes made by the religious establishment in similar circumstances, starting with the Crucifixion.'

'Really, Robin, I think that's in bad taste.'

'I feel my story shouldn't be brushed aside.'

'My defence to your charge is that I have heard it many times before. The voice of God is quite common, if I may be forgiven for saying so. I respect your intelligence, but would remind you that physical conditions often produce religious experiences, as I'm sure your research has revealed. Age, exhaustion, pain or simply overwork can summon up the gods. Shall we agree that time will tell whether your god is also mine?'

'You're saying I'll have to die to find out.'

'Yes – well – we all do – and that reminds me yet again of my next appointment. Goodbye, Robin – try to get some rest.'

Robin allowed himself to be ushered forcibly out of the vicarage and into the cheerless backstreet called St Columb's Row.

His heart fluttered. His heart was protesting. The interview had been a waste of possibly very precious time and precious energy. It had been nearly a quarrel, God was mocked, and Miss Woodly had probably missed the last rites by more than a whisker.

He thought of Tesco's, but, punningly although he was not amused, had not the heart for it. He might have prayed in St Columb's, but remembered that in the days of the do-gooders the doors had to be locked. He leant on his stick and made it to The Nest, where he rested until nearly lunchtime.

The telephone rang – another unexpected call – he was tempted not to answer – but the wild idea crossed his mind that it might be the Almighty on the line.

'Hullo?'

'Is that Robin?'

'Maybe. Who are you?'

'This is Dylan, Robin.'

'Do I know you?'

'You do. You should do. I'm your Father.'

'What?'

'Father Murphy, Dylan to you, your priest, your cousins' priest – begging your pardon, Robin, for my warped sense of humour.'

'Oh, Father Murphy – sorry!'

'Dylan, please.'

'Of course – Dylan.'

'Robin, I understand that you've been blessed with a revelation.'

'I don't know if I could or would call it that.'

'It's my longing to hear about it from your very own lips.'

'What was that?'

'Sorry, the Irish gets the better of me sometimes, I was meaning could we have a little chat?'

Robin smelt danger.

'Well,' he said.

'I know you're a Protestant, Robin, and that you have reservations respecting the Church of Rome. Let me assure and reassure you that I'm not out to snaffle a convert. From what I have gleaned from Maximilian, the Father of all of us has spoken to you from heaven, and I'm anxious and eager that myself and my flock should not be excluded from the wondrousness of such a happening in the midst of our humble community. Come and have tea with me, Robin, come today if you can, for I'm impatient to be in the company of a man recognised in an intimate manner by Himself. My housekeeper does a great tea, I can safely boast that she does.'

'I'm not very fit, Dylan.'

'That's a great pity.'

'And I'm rather a recluse.'

'Are you now! Robin, may I remind you that the Person who spoke to you is a healer? And He is and has been the saviour of many recluses in the holy monasteries and convents throughout history?'

'I know.'

'Of course you do – I'm teaching my grand-mother – there I go again! Please come to tea and I'll do my best to set things to rights.'

'That's very kind of you.'

'Is it yes?'

'Yes.'

'God be praised! Five o'clock at the Priest's House right beside St Mary's.'

Robin was ashamed even as he replaced the receiver. He had surrendered to sweet-talk. He had been seduced by suspect Irish blarney. He was almost a traitor to Protestantism, and not far enough from apostasy. Hubert Greenstock would be cut to the quick if he knew, or when he knew, how his parishioner was behaving. Robin himself felt like a commercial traveller, peddling his story to the highest bidder. On the other hand, he argued that it could not be wicked to enjoy being taken seriously and treated nicely for a change.

He ate a light lunch in order to have room for tea, and watched some of the children's programmes on TV – he was determined to ignore Hubert's advice about 'rest'.

When he rang the door chimes at the Priest's

House, the door was opened by a fine specimen of middle-aged womanhood, with flashing brown eyes and a smile that welcomed in spite of her discoloured teeth – Mrs Connolly.

Robin was taken aback when he held out his hand for her to shake and she raised it to her lips, saying: 'Pardon me, sir, for kissing the hand of the man who has been addressed by our Holy Father.'

Robin's apology of an answer was to grin and offer her the British Warm.

'How are you, sir, after such a tremendous shock?' Mrs Connolly asked.

'Quite well, thank you,' he replied.

'Fancy that!' She admired him for being quite well, not knowing he was actually quite ill. 'The Reverend's ready for you, sir.' He followed her into a comfy sitting-room with gas logs burning in the grate: another difference from Hubert Greenstock's hospitality.

The Reverend Dylan Murphy advanced towards his guest with open arms, but Robin restricted contact to a manly handshake.

Mrs Connolly announced from the doorway: 'I'll be leaving you two for a quarter of an hour, then I'll serve the "tay".'

Dylan Murphy gestured at her, shooing and smiling, and said to Robin: 'Thank you for your visit. Sit yourself down now, and spill the beans when you feel inclined.'

It was all light-heartedness and ease – Robin could not stop himself drawing comparisons. Dylan was about the same age as Mrs Connolly, and vigorous. His hair round his shaven circle of baldness, his tonsure, was dark. He wore corduroy trousers and a blue shirt with a black dicky in front connected with his white priestly collar. His cardigan lay on a chair. The furnishings of the room were a sofa facing the fire, chairs on either side of it, and a large TV set. There were flowers in a vase on the mantelpiece – they looked like woman's work.

Dylan remarked: 'You're a great writer, I've heard from your cousins.'

'Not a great one, and I'm inclined to think my cousins would confirm my opinion.'

'Come now, they're proud of you, Robin – they were proud even before you had been taken into the confidence of God. What's the title of the work in progress? I'll be wanting to buy a copy of the first edition.'

' "Progress" may be a misnomer, I fear. I've been struggling with the book for too many years to remember. But thank you for your interest. It was to be called *The Analogial Review of Religions.*'

'A deep subject, an expansive subject.'

'An expensive one, too – an expense of spirit – and not cheap in a monetary sense.'

'That's good, that play on words is music to my ears, it is – expansive, expensive – and exhausting, I shouldn't wonder – you're lucky to be a wordsmith, Robin!'

They discussed the English language and the Irish version of it. Dylan pursued the topic of Robin's 'magnificent' task. He spoke with admiration of the single-mindedness and loneliness of authorship. He ladled out the flattery.

At length Robin felt impelled to say in a repressive tone of voice: 'My book isn't finished and may never be. Recent events, one in particular, haven't helped. My book's looking more and more like a flop.'

'That's honest, that's modest – and I have to say I dearly love the ring of truth. But you will gain strength from your relationship with God – He will guide your hand until you write "The End" on the last page of your manuscript – doubt not, Robin!'

'Perhaps,' Robin replied, now wondering whether Hubert's chilling realism was not so bad.

'Will you tell me the true story I so long to hear?' Dylan asked.

Robin cut it short. He was inhibited by Dylan's gasps, eyes raised heavenwards, hands clasped as if in prayer, and signings of the cross. At the end of his recital he was embarrassed by Dylan suggesting a prayer and dropping on to his knees before the gas logs.

Mrs Connolly knocked and entered with one tray bearing a plate of slices of soda bread spread with butter and strawberry jam, and an iced chocolate layer-cake and a lardy cake, then returning with another tray of teapot, teacups and saucers, and plates, knives and spoons.

Robin said: 'I haven't seen such a tea for many years.'

Dylan said a snatch of 'grace': 'Oh well – for

what we are about to receive...' followed by an indulgent laugh.

He poured the tea and offered the edibles, and in due course, in a more businesslike manner, inquired: 'Have you corroboration of the sentence you were so privileged to hear?'

'Hubert Greenstock asked me the same question,' Robin replied. 'The answer seems to be no, but I still have to talk to Wendy Paddle.'

'Hubert's been sniffing around, has he?'

'I was with him this morning – it was my initiative.'

'What did he have to say to you, if I may be so bold as to ask?'

'He advised me to rest.'

'Were you satisfied with that advice? Did you consider your spiritual guide had been supportive?'

'I was disappointed.'

'Were you consigned to the category of poor hysterical persons who have thought through the ages they were walking and talking with God?'

'Yes.'

'Doesn't he know you're a brilliant man and wouldn't be misled by hoaxers?'

'He implied that my work is largely to blame for misleading me.'

'Were you in his study?'

'Yes.'

'I call it the confessional. People would confess to murdering their mothers in order to get out of it. He never switches on the second bar of that electric fire. Would I be exaggerating to suggest that he sent you away with a flea in your ear?'

'He meant well.'

'Hubert does, Hubert's an oak tree, English oak, and sometimes as thick as a plank of it. Listen, Robin! I recognise sincerity, and I believe in giving the benefit of the doubt to those who deserve it. I believe your story.'

'Thank you.'

'I'm honoured to be entertaining you. I count myself fortunate to be your neighbour. I don't know you well, but I can recognise a hero and nearly a saint when I see one – and don't deny it, Robin, that's what you must be to have merited the personal interest of the Almighty.'

'You're exaggerating – please stop!'

'Humility does you extra credit. The point is, the crux of the matter is – what are we to do with you?'

'Excuse me?'

'You are a gift from God, Robin, and it's up to us to turn you to the advantage of all of us.'

'I'm afraid I don't follow you.'

Dylan broke off to refill Robin's cup and to press him to more soda bread and accept a slice of the chocolate cake for future consumption.

'Our church differs from yours,' he resumed. 'You belong to a schismatic group, a splinter group, a sort of cult as a matter of fact, and whoever or whatever breaks away once will break away again. With respect, Robin, turncoats repeat themselves. I would point to differences between my church and yours. We Catholics love our church, whereas you Protestants seem mainly to want to rebel against yours. We are out to promote faith in Catholicism, the old original Christian church, and welcome all the breakaways back into the fold. And we would very much like to be associated with you in reinforcing the word of God.'

'How do you mean?'

'It would be a great start for you to preach in my church, Robin.'

'Oh no, I couldn't do that.'

'Do you have no feeling that you're indebted to His Holiness?'

'Oh dear, I don't think along such lines. I didn't ask God to shout at me.'

'But you say your prayers?'

'Yes – I do.'

'God answered them.'

'I never reckoned on strings being attached to my private religious leanings and dealings. And I never asked for what I've been given.'

'Did you not? If you'd wanted to steer clear of the limelight, would you have told the tale to your cousins? There's someone famous inside you, Robin, trying to get out.'

'No, no, you're mistaken – I'm a recluse.'

'Not for much longer or I'm a Dutchman. Our prayers have been answered whether or not yours have – you could boost our congregation at St Mary's. The next man to be God would attract a whole new crowd of worshippers. Raise up our church, Robin, and let our church protect you! I've spoken to my supervisors at the Cathedral in Westminster, and they would like you to do a sermon there.'

'Dylan, I'm horrified – none of this could possibly be the will of my God. I've said my say. How would or could the Roman Catholic church protect me?'

'Your story could have more chapters, Robin.'

'God forbid!'

'And my church is more versed in the way of the world than yours – we'd tuck you up in bed at night.'

'No – I'm a Protestant and I'm protesting. What happened to me is inexplicable, and the last thing I want is other people pretending to explain it. There must have been a mistake. I'm not a prince, I'm a failure. The message I received is a mystery, but to some extent nice for me. I won't have it chopped into little pieces by people with axes to grind, nor will I be a peepshow.'

'The wording of the message could be revised.'

'No, nothing doing, absolutely not – it would be fraudulent.'

'I hear you, Robin. Enough said. But don't forget my interest in your journeying, and the offers advanced that could be to your advantage.'

'Thank you, but I should be going.'

'Stay for the lardy cake!'

'I shouldn't.'

'Go on – be a devil for a change!'

8

The lardy cake lay heavily on his body and his conversation with Father Dylan Murphy lay heavily on his soul.

Tea at The Priest's House had been too good and the talk too bad, in Robin's puritanical opinions. He had felt trapped in Dylan's parlour. He now felt guilty. He either should not have accepted the invitation or he should have drawn lines through certain assumptions. He should not have let Mrs Connolly kiss his hand. He should have denied that he was holy with more force.

He plodded heavily back to The Nest – bird-like travel was out of the question. He made haste to his medicine chest and swallowed a cocktail of digestives. He sat in the armchair in his workroom, trying to sort out recollections of his religious day.

Hubert Greenstock had been as much use as a sick headache. He really had been hopeless. The mere mention of God on the telephone had put his hackles up. He had received the bearer of news about his Lord and Master, and his employer in a sense, with repeated warnings that he had no time to spare. All he had to offer Robin was doubt and dismissal.

That had happened in the morning. The afternoon had taken matters in the opposite direction. Dylan's mockery of Hubert's 'confessional' had persuaded Robin that the poor cold little room was more spiritual than the home comforts of The Priest's House. Mrs Greenstock, shy and retiring Dorothea, was known locally as the 'invisible woman': the descriptive adjective applied to Mrs Connolly was 'scarlet'. Robin's Catholic cousins had often complained that Father Murphy and Mrs Connolly looked happier together, parading round the parish, than the Greenstocks did, walking gravely here and there in single file.

As for Dylan's plans, they reminded Robin of his chapter in *The Analogical Review* dealing with religious skulduggery. He had proposed to amend the words that might have been spoken by the Almighty. He had said first that he was not out to nab Robin from the Church of England, and secondly that he wanted Robin to sermonise in the premises of the Church of Rome. He treated Robin like a trophy, or, more precisely, like an investment. He had prayed on his knees before tea for very much more than daily bread, he had prayed for cake and cash.

But whose fault was it that both religious professionals had behaved irreligiously?

Robin hesitated to distribute the blame further afield. His nerves rejected any more discussion of the vexing questions. He closed his eyes and, to the best of his ability, his mind. He thought of his dear mother, and soon drifted into sleep.

He woke in the dark, feeling cold. He was

cold, old and growing rapidly older. He was growing older as old people do, by disregarding the time-table of civilisation for going to bed, getting up and meals. He might have felt younger but for God. He would have felt better if he had not thrown himself on the mercy of the shepherds of the two flocks of local religious sheep.

He adjourned to the kitchen and lit the burners of his gas stove, also lit the oven and left the door open, in an attempt to warm himself. Explanations of his temperature occurred to him: winter weather; overheating as well as overeating in the Priest's House; the onset of the flu, or more serious illness; heretical stirrings that made his blood run colder still; and fears of being out of his depth. He wondered if he was freezing because of the folly of confiding in cousins and clerics and chatterboxes. Could it be that God was not amused by his antics and had rewritten His will?

He turned on the TV. It was a game show with money prizes. Watching it was preferable to searching his soul. Not long ago, when he had exercised his brain for hours on end, he was relaxed by the spectacle of brainlessness in action. But in the last few days he had broken rules and habits, and now felt uncomfortable with crass vulgarity.

He switched off the telly and noticed the time, eight o'clock, the hour at which his mother had sounded the gong for dinner. Robin was not hungry. He could fancy nothing but a Crunchie

– how long would he last without protein and vegetables? Who cared? He was experiencing the opposite of his rapture the other morning, paying the bill that nature submits for joy and often forgets to compensate for sorrow.

He took a dramatic decision. Early as it was, decadent as it might be, he would seek warmth and oblivion in bed.

He slept at once, before he was any warmer. He was woken by being as hot as he had been cold. He was boiling again, and something funny, or rather not funny, painful, was happening in his chest. The pain advanced and receded – rose and did not fall much – while he lay supine on the undersheet, uncovered, in his sopping pyjamas, not knowing what was going on or what to expect. Then his constitution seemed to change gear – he passed a sort of climax – was a little cooler – and dared to move gingerly. His heart was thumping on and off, but he was set on spongeing himself and putting on clean pyjamas. He reached the bathroom by clinging to furniture and stopping to recover his breath. Back in his bedroom, he placed his Jaeger dressing-gown on the wet bed and arranged himself on top of it, and pulled up the covers.

He slept no more. His heart kept jogging him awake. He thought of help and when he could receive it. He was unwilling to ring for an ambulance – he was not fit for hospitalisation. His future was either Scram's surgery at nine-thirty in the morning, or curtains. At some stage he switched on a light and looked at his wristwatch

– four o'clock, nearly four and a half hours before he could reach the heaven of medication.

He might have drowsed, or partially lost consciousness. At last the day dawned. His heart was still beating, whether or not as it should be. He was able to attend to his ablutions slowly. He ate some breakfast and walked to the Surgery and waited at the head of the queue of Doctor Ram's patients.

He was called in and said as he shut the door of the consulting room: 'I've had a heart attack.'

Scram was amused. He expostulated, 'My dear fellow!' and told Robin to 'park' himself on a chair. He asked questions, scribbled, peered at his computer. He tut-tutted when he took Robin's blood pressure and made his favourite joke before he sounded Robin's heart, 'Let's see what we can hear.'

'Well?' Robin queried.

'It's a mite wonky, and your blood pressure's a rascal.'

'In English, Scram?'

'You writers are so pedantic! I must refer you to a cardiac specialist and give you a prescription for a blood-thinner and increase your dosage of beta-blockers.'

'Does that mean I'm about to die?'

'Not bloody likely, as we say in England. Not just yet in my opinion, though I could be wrong. You were hot in the night and your heart's playing fast and loose. Maximilian tells me you have heard the voice of God. Was he joking?'

Robin hesitated – it could be asking for trouble to deny God.

'No,' he replied.

'Are you certain?'

'No one can say anything about God with certainty.'

'But you heard a voice?'

'I did.'

'I am most interested.'

'It's a long story.'

'But not a tall one?'

'Not to the best of my knowledge. Scram, my health – what's to be done?'

'Oh yes. We are in India no longer – you want action. Was the voice shocking?'

'I suppose so.'

'If you hear that voice again, please tell it not to meddle with the health of my patient. We will talk at greater length on another occasion. Are you feeling well enough to stay at home, or shall I try to get you into hospital?'

'I'm not bad.'

'If you are worse, ring for an ambulance. Here's your prescription.'

Robin, on the way out, said: 'Will I have to wait ages to see the specialist?'

'Not at all,' Scram returned, 'the specialist is married to my sister, he is my brother-in-law, his name is Walker, and he is not Indian.'

'Walker's not an Indian name.'

'Precisely. Listen – Harold Walker will see you chop-chop and he is to be trusted.'

Robin collected his pills from the Boroughfare

Pharmacy. Possession of them in their paper bag boosted at least his confidence, and he felt equal to shopping for food. Later, in The Nest, he was beset by a new problem.

It was the end of the week in which he had attracted supernatural attention. And custom and tradition ordained that he fed his cousin on Sunday evenings. But he had just treated Max to two meals: could he afford to entertain Max so soon again, afford either financially or emotionally?

He might not weather another storm of Max's mindlessness. Max chose to regard an encounter with God as one of Robin's attempts to establish his superiority over his cousin. Not only was Max's attitude grudging, mean, and almost blasphemous, it also influenced Zinnia and rendered her less likely to give Robin his dues of credit.

Robin swallowed some of his pills and decided to let Max go to bed hungry on Sunday. But Zinnia would not like that. Zinnia would not love him for punishing poor old hungry and thirsty Max. He wished he was back where he had been before he made the mistake of sitting on a bench in the Rec. Then he remembered that he had been suicidal at the time, and confusion upset his train of thought. He decided not to be decisive – he was not healthy enough to cope with the situations that had undermined his health, he would do the necessary later, when he had a clearer view of the way ahead.

He remembered his work. He had thought,

been told, read often, that work was the cure-all. He had had the experience of working previous difficulties out of his system. He went into his front room and his heart sank at the sight of those piles of paper on desks and tables.

He retreated strategically. He opted for work of a more modest type, housework. He made his bed and flicked his feather duster. He was washing his socks when he hit on a practical step towards elucidation of the mystery and the mitigation of attendant effects. He would talk to Wendy Paddle. She was the one potential witness of his transfiguration from an insignificant would-be historian of religion into a crypto-celebrity. If she had heard nothing, he could rule that he had been mistaken. In that case he would stop the gossip and rumours, and return to his point of departure – minus the death-wish and motivated to finish his book.

He ate a light lunch and about two-thirty donned his British Warm and pork-pie. He walked as jauntily as his stick allowed in the direction of Coronation Street, invigorated by his belated effort to help himself.

Jayendra Patel stood behind the counter close to the entrance of his newsagency-cum-mini-supermarket.

'Good afternoon, Mr Antrobus,' he said in his amiable manner.

'Good afternoon, Jayendra,' Robin replied, sorry to see a group of young children picking-and-mixing sweets from a display.

Sanjana, Mrs Patel, was also present in the

shop. She dressed Indian-style, in pretty saris, whereas Jayendra wore open-necked shirts and jeans. She stopped grubbing about in the freezer to call another greeting: 'All well, Mr Antrobus?'

'Fine, thanks,' Robin called back untruthfully: on top of his other troubles, he was disappointed not to be able to consult with Jayendra privately. 'Are you well, Sanjana?'

'We are on top of the world, sir,' she returned.

The Patels' policy was to address their customers formally and be addressed by their first names.

Jayendra inquired: 'What can I sell you, Mr Antrobus?'

'I'm not shopping at present, actually. No – I was wondering if you'd tell me how to contact your daughter?'

Jayendra's face clouded over.

'Indira is not in our good books,' he said.

'I know. I'm sorry about that. I wanted to ask her if she could or would do something for me.'

'What would that be, Mr Antrobus?'

'It's rather personal.'

They were interrupted. The children were queuing to pay for their sweets with pennies. Robin had to stand aside.

Jayendra resumed: 'I'm sorry, Mr Antrobus. What is this personal thing? My wife would be interested. May I include her?'

'Please!'

Jayendra bawled her name and Sanjana approached.

'Mr Antrobus wants our Indira,' Jayendra explained.

114

'Oh sir!' Her exclamation was a mixture of surreptitious snigger, rebuke and query. 'She is not even a pretty woman.'

Robin caught her drift and hurried to sort the matter out.

'I only want to ask her one question.'

'Are you wishing to propose or something, sir?'

'Propose? No! That is not my intention at all.'

Jayendra said: 'You sheltered under her umbrella, Mr Antrobus.'

Robin felt himself being dragged into deeper water.

'I would be grateful if your daughter could spare me two minutes of her time. It's a private matter, but I could speak to her in the shop.'

Jayendra had to attend to a customer.

Robin asked Sanjana: 'May I wait for her?'

'Oh yes, sir.'

'Her answer to my question would make a great difference to my life, you see.'

Sanjana looked puzzled, then said: 'She is training to be a beautician. It is not what we would like, and she is not very happy, although she is rebellious. She is a very kind girl, sir, and she is not stupid. She must settle down, it is true.'

'No doubt, no doubt,' Robin muttered, and hurried towards the shelves of magazines, most of which featured lewd women on their covers and might have confirmed the Patels in their misapprehensions.

His ten-minute wait also became embarrassing,

he had to buy Crunchies and a bottle of sherry, but at last the Patels' Indira and his Wendy entered, was spoken to by her father, smiled at him and approached with her small beringed hand outstretched.

She was quite plain, her eyebrows met and her nose was sharp, the granny glasses halfway down her nose did not help, the same applied to a white streak in her long straight black hair, and her western clothes seemed not to suit her. But her smile was open and her handshake was bold and firm.

'Good day, Mr Antrobus,' she said. 'How can I serve you?'

Robin flinched at her choice of words, but guided her gratefully along to a quieter corner of the shop where the 'liquids' and the other cleaning products were stocked.

'You remember,' he began; 'Wendy, you remember when we met in the Rec during the storm on Monday afternoon?'

'Yes, sir.'

'Where were you walking from, if I may ask?'

'I live down in Kilburn. I share a flat with other girls. My studies finish at one o'clock, I'm free most afternoons, and do work experience in a beauty salon evenings. In the afternoons I often come here to buy food for all three of us – it's cheaper. I walk from the Tube across the Rec.'

'Thank you. I see. There was a thunderstorm, wasn't there?'

'I'll say!'

'And a clap of thunder?'

116

'I didn't notice.'

'A very loud, noticeably loud, clap of thunder a few minutes before you saw me by that bench?'

'I could have been too far away.'

'But you knew it was a thunderstorm?'

'I sure did. Is the thunder important, Mr Antrobus?'

'Yes, but it's not the most important thing.'

'What's more important?'

'A voice.'

'Sorry?'

'A loud man's voice, did you hear it?'

'What was it saying? Whose voice was it?'

'You didn't hear it?'

'I can't say yes, sir. Could you tell me a little more?'

'Wendy, forgive me for asking, do you have a friend, a boy, who lives near the Rec and dabbles in electronics?'

'Yes and no.'

'But you know him?'

'He's my parents' friend.'

'I have to be more inquisitive – I'll explain later – can I ask a very inquisitive question? Don't answer if you don't want to.'

'I'm ready, sir.'

'Is he your boyfriend, does he want to be your boyfriend?'

'My parents are trying to make me marry him.'

'Good heavens!'

'I won't.'

'Is he a bad boy?'

'No – but I do not marry to order, I do not!'

'I mean, does he play tricks? Would it have been like him to project a loud voice across the Rec to tease you or frighten you?'

'He's clever but a fool, and I guess he could not do anything so clever as you describe. He surely could not. Would you let me ask you a question, sir?'

'Of course.'

'When you were under my umbrella you weren't feeling well, I think. Was it because of that voice?'

'Probably, yes.'

'Was it religious, sir?'

A customer came between them, needing help to find a product called Clean Sweep.

Robin said: 'How do you know that? How did you guess that?'

'When you were under my umbrella you asked if I was religious.'

'Did I?'

'If you weren't feeling right, was it because of a shock that had something to do with religion?'

'Perhaps I shouldn't keep you talking, Wendy, because you've already told me what I had to know, and your parents would like to get rid of me.'

'You said you'd explain, sir. I'm inquisitive, too.'

'The voice seemed to come from the sky.'

'Gosh!'

'I don't know, nobody knows, who it belonged to.'

118

'A religious person, was it?'

'Yes.'

'A ghost?'

'Not exactly.'

'What did he say?'

'He referred to the Christian religion.'

'I'm reading the Christian Bible. I'm looking for a religion that isn't Islam.'

'It's a secret, Wendy.'

'You could trust me, sir, but you might not believe that you could.'

'It's not such a big secret. Cousins of mine have been blabbing it round the town. The voice told me this: "You are the crown prince of my kingdom." Do you understand?'

'The kingdom is God's?'

'Yes.'

'It was God, sir?'

'You didn't hear it. My writings are all to do with religion. I must have dreamed that God spoke to me. The story probably boils down to meaning my imagination was playing tricks. You couldn't have missed hearing that voice if it had been real. Nobody heard it but me. Silly nonsense, Wendy! I'm sorry I've bothered you.'

'What an experience, sir!'

'Yes.'

'You are next to God, it informed you?'

'Yes.'

'It could be true, Mr Antrobus.'

'No, Wendy.'

'I would prefer to think it true – it would be safer.'

'That's a point. I must go.'

'Sir, could I talk to you about God?'

'I'm not a priest, Wendy – you'd do much better to talk to a priest.'

'My work is not suitable. I study beautification in a temporary manner. Not being a Muslim any more is difficult. My life will be easier when I belong to another religion. I need God, not a husband, Mr Antrobus.'

'Yes, yes, well ... I'm sure you will find Him, or He will find you, when the time comes.'

'Sir, will you tell me if God speaks to you again?'

'I'm afraid He won't. It may be better for all concerned if He doesn't. But I promise to tell you if He does.'

'Thank you, sir. Is that all?'

'Yes. Thank you, Wendy. Good luck with your future. Goodbye, my dear.'

They shook hands. Robin was touched by the girl's serious and sincere brown eyes searching his face for godly traces. He was sad for a variety of reasons, not least that he had nothing to say or to offer such a clever person. He turned away and walked towards the exit, where Jayendra and Sanjana were waiting.

'Was it satisfactory, sir?' Jayendra inquired.

'Your daughter does you credit,' Robin replied.

Sanjana asked: 'Have you finished with her, sir?'

'Oh yes – yes – but I think we are friends.'

Sanjana was more critical of her daughter than Jayendra had been.

'She is wasting her youth, Mr Antrobus. She does not know her luck. She should marry, she should – we know the right husband for her. And if she won't, she should be a solicitor – she has the qualifications for that. Now she offends her parents.'

'Wait and see,' Robin told her. 'You'll be proud of her one day, I expect.'

He walked home. He was relieved as well as sad. He rang up Max.

'Am I interrupting the company doctor in his surgery?' he inquired.

Max bit back.

'God knows – hasn't He told you what I'm doing?'

'Sorry, Max – pax, Max – will you have dinner with me on Sunday?'

9

That evening Robin received a telephone call. He was scared of answering it – his nerves were not in good shape, however healthy his body might or might not be.

'Hullo?' he blurted out between fear and breathlessness.

'Is that Mister Robin Antrobus?'

'Speaking.'

'I'm Harold Walker, Dr Walker. You're Dr Ram's patient, and he's asked me to check you over. Can you be at Southwood Hospital at nine tomorrow morning?'

'But it's Sunday...'

'I work on Sundays.'

'Oh yes – yes, I can.'

'Southwood Hospital, near the Tube, nine tomorrow morning – see you then.'

'Thank you.'

Robin was grateful to Scram, even if his evening was ruined, and his night disturbed. On the other hand he liked Dr Walker's brisk efficiency. The last thing he wanted was an inefficient surgeon.

He caught a Metropolitan Line train at Boroughfare station at eight o'clock in the morning. He had crossed the Rec and come to no harm. He reached Southwood and found the hospital, got through the paperwork and joined the crowd in the waiting area. A nurse called his name on the dot of nine and ushered him into a consulting room. Dr Walker was a nice-looking man, but Robin wished he had not been wearing his operating gear, green skull cap and loose green overall.

Dr Walker explained his attire in a ghoulish way: 'I'm going to have to do some plumbing in a quarter of an hour' – meaning bypass surgery.

On the other hand he was chatty while he took notes, tested pulse and blood pressure, listened with his stethoscope to Robin's heart and fixed electrodes to Robin's torso.

He said Scram had two unpronounceable Indian first names, and that all the family, even his sister Jankti, Dr Walker's wife, used his nickname.

He referred to Robin's literary activities.

'I understand that you write about religion and may have had a religious experience.'

Robin was dismissive: 'The experience was a storm in a teacup in several senses.'

'Do you think it made you feel ill?'

'Well, it's been rather a stressful time.'

'Are you feeling better now?'

'Oh yes.'

'Back to normal?'

'Absolutely.'

'Quite sure?'

'Quite.'

'Well done!'

Robin put on his shirt and tie, and clambered into his old tweed jacket, while Dr Walker looked at the print-out of his electrocardiogram.

'Sit yourself down,' Dr Walker said.

Robin did so.

Dr Walker said: 'You have a good doctor, Mr Antrobus. Scram was right to send you along to me. But I'm pleased to tell you with some certainty that you haven't suffered cardiac infarction, as we call it nowadays – no heart attack.'

'What a relief!'

'Yes ... But – another but – with apologies – you have a weakness in your heart. I'm not surprised that it caused you some of the symptoms of a heart attack, I'm only amazed that you have not suffered similar symptoms in the past. Further tests are next on the agenda, and promptly. I'm giving you a prescription for a pill to put under your tongue if and when the trouble repeats itself. Should the pill not afford you relief, ring at once for an ambulance, which will take you to the nearest Accident and Emergency. In due course I'll then be contacted. Now I must say goodbye. Nurse will bleed you on your way out and fix another appointment. Goodbye, Mr Antrobus.'

Robin was shocked. He was taken aback. Suddenly, within the space of seconds, his spirits had risen to higher than high and plummeted to lower than low. Of course his heart was weak – he was a weakling – he had really known it all along. The question was, the most important question, unanswered, was: how weak? Dr Walker should have postponed his 'plumbing' and provided more information.

He had his precious blood taken and was given in exchange another threatening appointment. He was eventually able to don his British Warm and get out into air that did not smell sinister. He walked to Southwood station, trying to come to terms with the fact that he was iller than he had assumed he was. The two platforms, the up one and the down, were underground, and now almost deserted. Somebody clattered on the stairway and must have been catching a train on the down side, for central London. On Robin's platform only an old lady with shopping bags sat on a bench at a distance from where he stood and waited. The down train squeaked to a halt and clanked away, and relative silence fell.

A breeze or a draft, the air pushed forwards by a train on its way, swirled and whooshed on to the platform, followed by increasingly loud metallic noises issuing from the black hole of the relevant tunnel.

And Robin distinctly heard that deep voice – it was slowly saying: 'Teach the people.'

He reeled. His train came in. A guard or the driver was asking him if he was all right. He said he would sit on the bench vacated by the old lady. He was helped to it, and the train pulled out.

'Oh no,' he was saying to himself. 'Oh no – not today of all days – no, no!'

Was he growing hot? Was he going to have a

heart attack? He did not have pills for it – he had not yet had the prescription dispensed. How was he to call an ambulance? How would the ambulance men get him up the steps? He would prefer not to pass over where he was – he was even amused to think that he might be going 'down the tubes', as modern jargon could or would refer to his possible fate.

A second thought crossed his mind. He had no pain. He had no symptoms. His heart not only beat regularly; in another sense it was uplifted. He seemed to have been more wrong than ill. For he had doubted, sought evidence as if for a crime, acted the scientist, and allowed himself to be swayed by ignoramuses and cynics. He was alone on the platform, yet not lonely. This time no trick could have been played on him. He had been commanded not to throw in his lot with those in the scriptures who were approached by God and knew Him not. He had not only been addressed a second time by divinity, by divine means, by some being inexplicable except in terms of religion, but had also been given a mission.

The next train for Boroughfare came in. He boarded and sat down. Was he meant to inform the oily youth sitting with his legs wide apart, and the old gent reading the deaths column in *The Times*, and a harassed mother jamming a dummy into her baby's mouth, and the woman and probably her daughter quarrelling in undertones, that he was appointed by God to teach them – teach them what? – to be good people, better than they were, sorry they had been naughty, and to hurry to church?

He giggled inside. Such an uncharacteristic proceeding would surely not be the sort of thing that was required. His excitement resembled his previous experience of rapture – both were short-lived. He landed with a bit of a bump on *terra firma*.

Could that vocal instruction have actually been an aberration of one of his little grey cells? Could God be in his head too truly? And if not, what then?

Earth seemed to be a grubby fretful place after his momentary soar above it. He was nearly at Boroughfare station and was going to have to run the gauntlet of the Rec: would God issue another tall order? Questions encircled him. To put it another way, he was not far from drowning in deeper and deeper water.

He arrived at Boroughfare and joined the stampede for the escalator. What would the people say if he should bellow that he was appointed by God to give them a sharp lesson? He searched the sky as he set foot on the tarmac path trodden by Wendy Paddle under her umbrella. There was no sign of a storm. The day was still and relatively quiet. He took longer steps and his proximity to Roebuck Buildings twanged another of his nerves.

He thought of Max. He was reminded that he had invited Max to supper. Memories taunted and tortured him. He had ridiculed the idea that the Almighty had plans for him and announced them in advance of their implementation. And he had denied a God who was capable of making Himself heard on earth. He had suggested God was silly. But he had been the silly one to cast aspersions while his heart was on the blink.

He hurried to the emergency pharmacy in Coronation Street, run by Mr and Mrs Wates, both slow-coaches in their seventies, and begged them to give him his pills without delay. Half an hour later he was able to take cover in The Nest. He divested himself of his outdoor clothes and slumped into the chair in his workroom. The emotions of the morning had exhausted him. He held on to his bottle of pills and drifted towards sleep, wondering if he would wake up.

But he did wake. He woke at one o'clock, lunch time, feeling hungry. He was the recipient of good news as well as bad, he reflected, he had been honoured again, singled out for divine attention, and he cooked himself a possibly strengthening if unhealthy meal, a pork chop, chips and peas, all frozen. Afterwards, after eating it, he rang Zinnia.

She answered the telephone with a monosyllabic coo: 'Yes?'

Robin spoke.

'Oh, it's you,' she said irritably. 'Why aren't you a tasty young barrister I want to ask to dinner.'

'Sorry,' Robin said. 'As a matter of fact I'm asking you to dine. Would you have dinner this evening?'

'Good gracious, Robin! Have you come into money?'

'You and Max think of nothing but money. There's something more to discuss.'

'Is it religious?'

'In a way.'

'Max told me you'd seen the light and realised that you won't be His Nibs.'

'None of that's accurate, Zinnia. Do come! I need to bring you up to date, and advice.'

'Are you okay, Robin?'

'Fairly.'

'What's wrong?'

'I'll explain.'

'Will we be alone?'

'No, Max is coming.'

'Damn!'

'Please, Zinnia.'

'Oh, very well. Usual time and place?'

'Yes.'

'I could have guessed.'

She rang off.

Robin braced himself, and at length, after dawdling and procrastinating, went and looked more seriously at all that existed of his *Analogical Review*, the reams of notes, memos, lists, drafts and fairer copies, and the very much smaller pile of typescript. He had stored some of his research in cheap paper files of different colours. Up to twenty such bulging files, blue, pink, green, cream, yellow, were placed one on top of another in stacks. They bore inscriptions: Judaism, Roman Catholicism, Protestantism, Marxism and so on. Here, near his antiquated typewriter, was his introduction to his book, defining the word analogy and explaining that his intention was to seek out new truths by means of comparing religions and relating them to national circumstances, the character of races, and the influences of climate and diet.

He was never a fluent writer, let alone a prolific one. He had suffered from all the inhibitions that literary work is heir to. He always cringed to have to commit himself on paper. He dreaded criticism. He had embarked on the *Review* almost convinced that he would not finish it. And Dr Walker had now put a stopper on the book, his ambitions, his capabilities.

Yet God apparently demurred. God might be looking forward to Robin's demise, judging by His offer of a good time in the next world, but he had also ordered Robin to do a pedagogic job that could not be considered short-term. The crux of the matter was as old as the hills or even older: what was He driving at?

Robin sought answers to his questions throughout the rest of Saturday and on Sunday until his doorbell rang at seven-thirtyish. He was more relieved to see Zinnia and Max than he ever had been – at least their faces were not mysterious.

They exchanged greetings, walked to Ab's Caf, sat where they always sat, and ordered the same meal with a bottle of wine.

Zinnia took the bull by the horns in a far-fetched manner of speaking.

'What's new, Robin?'

'I don't know where to start. Are both of you all right?'

Heads were nodded.

'How's business?' Robin asked Max.

'On the slow side,' Max replied, munching his roll and butter.

'Spill the beans, Robin,' Zinnia said.

'I've had a scare.'

'Who's scared you?'

'That's not the point. I had a bit of a heart attack.'

'What bit was that?' Max asked.

Zinnia was more sympathetic.

'When did this happen?'

'I'm afraid I'm losing track of time.'

'What did it feel like?'

'Hot – I boiled – but it didn't last long.'

'How long is long?' Max inquired.

Robin ignored him and said: 'I saw Scram, who referred me to his brother-in-law who's a cardiac specialist.'

'I didn't know Scram had a sister, let alone a brother-in-law,' Max said.

'She's called Jankti.'

'Funny name.'

'Well, it's Indian.'

'It would be, so would she, I suppose.'

'Oh Max!'

Zinnia demanded: 'What did the specialist say?'

'That I'd had a kind of rehearsal for a heart attack. He wanted a sample of my blood, and I've an appointment for more exhaustive tests.'

'Poor Robin!'

Max weighed in.

'You don't want to take these little upsets seriously.'

'My heart's peculiar.'

'What's that?'

'There's something wrong with it.'

'Who says so?'

'Dr Walker.'

'He could be a quack. Did you yourself give him the idea?'

'He took an electrocardiogram.'

'You can't trust those machines. Believe me! I've got stones in my gall bladder, that's a fact, however often x-rays and scans deny it. I know a hell of a lot about illness, worse luck! And I'm ready to bet your heart's as sound as a wedding bell.'

Zinnia said: 'Max, I do wish you'd shut up. You get everything wrong, even wedding bells – they're electronic nowadays and usually go wrong. Robin, what's the name of your specialist?'

'Dr Walker, Harold Walker.'

'Is he good? Where did you see him?'

'At Southwood Hospital. He seems to be important there. He's a surgeon.'

'What else did he say about your condition?'

'He thought I was lucky.'

'Lucky to have had a heart attack?'

'Lucky to be alive.'

'Did he think you were in danger?'

'He gave me a prescription for stuff to suck if there was another crisis.'

'Sweets?'

'No – pills – pills to put under my tongue – pills that should calm down the heart.'

'What if they don't?'

'He told me to call an ambulance.'

'Sounds like cold comfort.'

'Well, Dr Walker fitted me in at short notice – he was busy even on a Sunday morning – he isn't one of those surgeons without patients that nobody wants to be cut up by – and he explained that he'd understand my heart better after the next tests.'

'Did you like him?'

'Yes – as much as one can like a doctor who bears news that isn't good.'

'Oh Robin!'

Zinnia was concerned, and, as Ab and Debra arrived with the food, she caught hold of Robin's forearm and gave it a squeeze.

Max, having picked up his knife and fork, clutched them pointing upwards in his hands as he delivered himself of the following.

'Here's my opinion, and you should both darn well listen to it, because I have reason to know health better than you do. I've read my medical dictionary, unfortunately, and my diagnosis is that Robin's on the mend. He'll be tops, if not A1. Why? I'll tell you why. Hearing voices is harmful. His heart's paying his mind back for assuming that God was going to whip him up to heaven and welcome him with open arms. Your ambitions ran away with you, Robin, and have damn nearly made you ill. You use your common sense, and Dr Walker will congratulate you on getting your ticker to keep time. What I'm saying is, thank the Lord for persuading you to drop all the religious nonsense!'

Max attacked his escalope, and Zinnia asked Robin: 'Is that true? Don't you believe any more that God spoke to you.'

'Not true.'

'What?'

'Things have changed.'

'What things?'

'God.'

'The whole point of God is that He doesn't change. What are you saying, Robin?'

'I don't know if God's involved, but I've had another message.'

'What was it?'

' "Teach the people".'

Max dropped his knife and fork on his plate, whether by accident, because he was so surprised, or by design, to communicate exasperation.

'That's a tough assignment,' Zinnia said.

'Yes.'

'What are you going to teach them? What are you going to teach us?'

'I don't know.'

'Where did you hear the voice? Was it in the Rec again?'

'No, in the Tube. I was on the platform, waiting for a train.'

'What station?' Max asked.

'Southwood.'

'What were you doing there?'

'I've told you – seeing Dr Walker at Southwood Hospital.'

Zinnia again took charge.

'Where did the voice come from?'

'Inside the tunnel, as the train was coming in – it might have had something to do with the air that's pushed along by the train.'

'Was it any help?'

'What do you mean?'

'After being told about your heart?'

'No – no and yes – it worried me – it's worried me so much that I've hardly thought of my heart.'

'No wonder.'

'What am I to do?'

'God knows!'

'True, but ... I asked you to have dinner partly because I wanted advice.'

Max cleared his throat and said: 'I can't see you in a mortarboard and gown, Robin – they wouldn't suit you.'

Zinnia rebuked him: 'Don't be stupid! Schoolmastering's nothing to do with it. Nor are you, for that matter.' She turned to Robin. 'Your book's a teaching text, isn't it – or will be?'

'My book's in the doldrums and it's been overtaken by events.'

'But it's history, a history of religions, and your record of the past must be factual and permanently valid.'

'History isn't like that. It can record a birth and a death, but the rest is open to interpretation – it's up for grabs, as they say. Every history, every interpretation of it, is transient, and especially so where religion's the subject. I don't fancy the idea of God looking over my shoulder when I write about Him, and grinding His teeth over my mistakes. I'd rather not have the feeling

135

that I was either being patted on the back or punished by the ultimate headmaster.'

'Are you threatening to give up?'

'I'm afraid my book's been knocked on the head, as I have.'

'You've taken so long, Robin – we've waited so long – don't let your life go to waste.'

'Oh well – my heart will certainly rule my head in this context.'

'No – I can't stand defeatism – you're not to be passive – I'm not taking the mixture as before – teach your book if you can't or won't write it!'

They were interrupted. Debra collected their plates, and Max drew attention to Ab and his offer of desserts. Zinnia and Robin plumped for vanilla ices, and Max had the Peach Melba – they were all conservatives.

Max again weighed in.

'Who's behind these messages you're getting, and what's behind them, is as clear as mud. Personally, I regard both as twaddle. On the other hand, I could be wrong. Yes, I could, for once.' The others laughed. 'If they're kosher – oh, sorry, I shouldn't use that word, especially in this restaurant – I'll start again: if they happened to come from above, in case they have, you take my advice, Robin, and do as you've been told by my sister.'

'No.'

'Yes, Robin,' Zinnia chimed in. 'Give a talk, not a sermon in church, a little lecture in my flat, one evening, for our friends.'

'What could I say?'

'Speak the truth and shame the devil! Abridge your book, pick out a few juicy bits, be yourself!'

'Honestly, I don't want to.'

'That's unlike you, that's selfish. Look here, Robin! Supposing you're not what you used to be, you're an exception, and you have been or will be glorified – just supposing – your cousins, your only relations, are surely entitled to reflections of the glory. Do it for us, please – we're people, your people – God's bound to be pleased, whether or not His finger's in the pie – and it'll be a party, the first party we've had since we were children and no doubt the last, and, with a little more luck than we're used to, a happy occasion.'

10

'It wasn't my idea,' Robin began his speech to the
company assembled in Zinnia Jones's living-room.
The priests Greenstock and Murphy were present;
also the Patels, Jayendra in a knee-length white
garment, Sanjana in a scintillating Sari, sitting
with Wendy Paddle, who wore a Union Jack T-
shirt and jeans; also Scram from the Surgery and
Ab from the Caf; and Robin's neighbours, Rhoda
and Ruth Padger in old-fashioned hats, and Bill
Rickitt, displaying his hefty bare arms with tattoos.
About a dozen other people had been invited by
Zinnia and Max. It was seven in the evening of
a chill November day, and Robin had been intro-
duced by Zinnia and asked to stand up. He held
some sheets of paper in his obviously shaky right
hand, and smiled at everyone in a shy and pained
manner.

'None of this was my idea,' he said. 'I'm not
a public speaker or a public anything. I really
don't know what to say, except that I'm sorry.
Oh dear! It must be a mistake to start by
apologising – sorry again!

'I can't quite agree with the title that's been
pinned on to my talk. "Living with God" doesn't
sound right to me. I have nothing to boast about.

But, although it's inaccurate and bad English, I suppose it's a half-truth.

'What's half-true about it is that I've spent most of my life trying to write commentaries on religion. I could admit to being a student of theology, an amateur in the sense of having been drawn to the subject, and a professional inasmuch as I've worked exclusively in response to my calling for many years.

'Religion's rather a daunting word. Theology's more so. English people have always run a mile from words like those. They probably run farther and faster today, since our country's become pagan. But God's older than paganism. God's older than religion and theology. God may have created man, man certainly created God. As soon as our forefathers realised they had been born and would die, they found or made God usually in their own image.

'Religion's our antidote to death. That was its beginning. It offers a form of afterlife. It promises to cure sickness and sorrow. It's glad tidings to the poor of every description. It lends us courage. It's hope. It's beauty.

'It's atheism, too. You cannot deny God until you've thought of Him. Atheists need God to authorise their claim that they can do without Him. Atheists seek a substitute for God. They disgraced themselves in the last century, the twentieth century, by swapping God for communism and worshipping their idol, Lenin. Communism still has to answer the charge that in practice it was devil worship.

139

'Some golden calves are more golden than others. Marx, Lenin, Stalin, and their African and Asian counterparts, Pol Pot, for example, deserve less attractive epithets. Our pagan compatriots bow and scrape before the graven image of affluence. Affluence is good for people, but bad for God. Affluence and the Welfare State are like the waters of Lethe, the river in Greek mythology, a draft of which causes forgetfulness. They are not a human right. Money – savings, charitable institutions – cannot be counted on. Thieves and politicians can steal it. Its value is dependent upon extraneous and uncontrollable forces.

'And hard times always arrive. And God's patience is rewarded by our problems. Hard times for a country resemble the proximity of death for an individual. Catastrophes happen, wars are fought, bodies bleed, hearts are broken, money goes west, health is fragile, science fails us, death beckons – who can help, except the Almighty?

'Yet religion's not necessarily the adjunct of gloom. We're religious against a rainy day. We're religious in hopes of being led to the sunny uplands of earth or heaven. Religion comforts and consoles, and promises and pledges that we have more reason to embrace joy than submit to sorrow.

'Forgive my long-windedness and egoism, please! No doubt I'm not so faithful as I should be, for I've always had to redefine religion and what it means to me and to others, so that I could be convinced that my work was worthwhile.

140

And now I have laid my redefinition to the best of my ability before you.

'My book, yes – some of you have kindly taken an interest in it. Still more kindly, they have not on the whole accused me of dragging my feet, or malingering. Alas, it's not finished yet. Owing to personal factors, I wonder if I shall ever finish it. No matter – too many books are written and published nowadays and too few read! When my cousin Zinnia first suggested I ought to do a talk – neither sermon nor lecture – I refused. Then it was put to me that, if I couldn't write my book, I should pick out bits and proffer them to anyone willing to lend an ear.

'That's why we're here this evening, inescapably in my case though not in yours – I promise I shall not object if any of you walk out.

'Well, to begin at the beginning, or more precisely not to begin there, my researches skipped through the stirrings of religion in the people who emerged from the primeval slime. Incidentally, does the primeval slime remain part of science's ghastly alternative to the delightful *Book of Genesis*?

'However, although savagery is not a pleasant phase of our history, it foreshadows a lot of modern notions, mistakes, practices, crimes and sins.

'Our species has had a weakness for power, human and especially divine power from the word go. Savages attributed it to objects, locations, animals, persons, and called their gods by different names. They have bequeathed to later generations one of those unanswerable questions, called "teasers" by Judaism: what is the difference between superstition and religion?

'Harking back to genesis, our origins, not the *Book*: I don't like to have my nose rubbed in the possibility that we're descended from chimps. I prefer not to believe it. But it's troubling to see chimps behaving as inquisitively and frivolously as human beings, and human beings behaving as callously as chimps. The worst news to emerge from the comparison of our race with chimps is that we are even nastier and more bloodthirsty and murderous than they are. The Russian people would have been happier if they had made a chimp their leader after the October Revolution.

'Early religionists took an unhealthy interest in the orifices of the human body. They also sought religious inspiration in alcohol, drugs, orgies of dancing, sacrifices of whatever or whoever was of the greatest value and would therefore gain more godly favour. Blood was soon on the sacrificial menu: the Aztecs in Mexico thought their gods would be pleased to watch the blood of virgins cascading down a pyramidal structure.

'I was going to say I would draw another veil over the primitive religions of the Middle East and India, but they are already veiled by aeons of time, by holy numbers, seven, ten and twelve, and by enigmatic symbolism.

'Ancestral religions seem secretive to us, and perhaps always were. Consider the Chinese religion or way of life known as Confucianism: its founder,

142

born in 551 BC, was called K'ung Chu, also Kung Fu Tzu, Kong Fuzi, Kung Zi, and his *nom-de-plume* was Chung Ni. Confucianism is confusing, I would have to say with respect; but a certain ambiguity in its tenets might have been created to suit the genius of the Chinese people.

'What a pity the Church of England forgot to remember that all religions have to be mysterious – how can they be otherwise? – and produced a new translation of the Bible that attempts to change mystical poetry into the prose of a government announcement!

'Christianity came along five hundred years after Confucius, and Islam came six hundred years later. I couldn't possibly discuss Christianity here, in front of two ministers of Christ. I hope they will forgive me for only mentioning some intriguing and lesser known historical facts.

'Jesus did not, and said he did not, build Christianity from scratch. Christianity is a development of previous faiths – of Judaism, and Mithraic ceremonies involving bread, and the spring rites of other religions promising resurrection. The images of the Great Mother, and the child born of the Divine Virgin, derive from the religions of Babylonia and the Hellenistic Period.

'The Gospels were probably written not by disciples, but by one or more committees, and must be the most successful example of such work. I was touched to find out that the word in the Gospels by which Jesus addresses his heavenly Father, *Abba*, approximates in English to "daddy". The point is that He taught his

143

fellow-Jews, and those who had been taught entertained no idea of the informalities of His message reaching beyond the Jewish congregation. It was St Paul who allowed gentiles into the Christian fold.

'A statistic informs us that nowadays there are 1,000,000,000 Christians, believe it or not. Statistics are human, therefore disagree. Another informs us that there are 22,000 sub-divisions and sects of the Christian religion. What a rocky road has been trodden over two thousand years of its history! Christians have withstood their differences of opinion, attacks by enemies from without and within, errors galore and the Reformation. They have weathered the storm of intellectual evaluations and commentary, of criticism, of definitions of essence and identity, of Teilhard de Chardin's "Omega Point" when the world is saved, and goodness knows what else devised by scholars and sophisticates. A unifying factor has been and remains the aspiration to be eligible for admission to a heaven of some sort.

'A strange thing is that while the Princes of the Church, the Popes and Archbishops, and the devoutest and cleverest representatives of their flocks throughout twenty centuries, wrangled and wrote learned tomes about the Christian ideal here on earth, the consensus was and still is to become simply "a child of God", which is not far removed from "the mindless sage" of Zen Buddhism.

'Buddhism is four or five hundred years older

than Christianity. The Buddha and Confucius were almost contemporaries. The liberalism of their relatively gentle religions has attractions for western seekers for some not too difficult rule to live by. But I haven't studied them deeply as yet; and the same applies to Islam, the Muslim religion. Whether or not I could or should venture into those regions is a moot point – the East is another country also in a religious sense, and I am not political.

'Granted, Christianity began in the East, the Middle East. But the frozen North seems to have fashioned it over the years into the fitting occupant of Gothic cathedrals. If or when English people are no longer affluent and luck runs out, I rather doubt that they will turn to foreign faiths.

'I think that's all I have to say. Thank you so much for listening to me.'

Robin sat down. His audience began to clap in a startled and subdued manner. Zinnia raised her voice.

'Don't stop! Don't be silly, Robin! That's not the end.'

Max chimed in.

'Buck up, Robin – we've only had the *hors d'oeuvres!*'

The three cousins began to mutter at one another in a huddle, members of the audience were consulting as to what they were meant to do, and an authoritative voice with an Irish accent rang out.

'We're not getting our money's worth,' Dylan Murphy said inaccurately, for no money had changed hands. 'We were expecting something more dramatic, Robin.'

Hubert Greenstock prepared to depart.

'I've heard enough, Robin,' he said with a hint of asperity. 'Thank you and your cousins.'

There was uncertain murmuring, and chairs were pushed about.

A girl spoke.

'Mr Antrobus, please tell your God story.'

It was Wendy Paddle. Some people giggled at her phraseology.

Robin looked round, spotted her, smiled at her and replied: 'All right.'

He again stood and faced his audience. Hubert Greenstock changed his mind and sat. Silence fell gradually.

'I decided not to tell that story. I hoped I wouldn't have to. I didn't mean to give this talk, but I have, so I might as well carry on. Father Murphy and Wendy Paddle and my cousins know that I had an odd experience the other day. I received a message from the sky, or thought I did. I'm choosing my words as carefully as I can, because I'm making no claims and trying my best not to offend anyone.'

He paused. He was very red in the face and not breathing well.

'I'm sorry,' he said.

'Don't stop there,' Max shouted.

'No – all right – the voice said "You are the crown prince of my kingdom" – it was like the voice of Bambi's father in the Disney film. I suppose the message referred to the kingdom that figures in the Lord's Prayer. Why I received such a message is beyond me. I'm an insignificant person. And my interest in religions is academic rather than pious. I don't deserve to be favoured by the Almighty. Furthermore, Jesus was and understood that He was the son and heir of his Father.'

Zinnia now filled a momentary pause by urging Robin to continue.

'There was only one possible witness – I mean the only one I know about – who was in the Recreation Ground during or soon after I heard the voice. Yes, I had been sitting in the Rec when the storm broke – did I omit to say that? The clouds parted in a theatrical way and the voice came through, as if magnified by a loudhailer. Anyway, my witness, a young friend of mine, heard nothing of relevance. Auto-suggestion or something of that sort must have played a trick on me.'

Robin smiled at his audience pleadingly. He was pleading to be allowed to say no more.

But Zinnia said: 'No, Robin, you won't get away with it. If you won't, I will!'

He capitulated.

'I've heard the voice again,' he said. 'It spoke to me out of a tunnel at Southwood Tube Station – I was on the platform, waiting for a train. An old woman was also waiting, but she cannot have heard anything out of the ordinary, for she got on to the train that arrived. Perhaps the second episode, and the first for that matter, were more funny than anything else. The message at Southwood was "Teach the people".'

147

Father Murphy asked a question.

'Have you been teaching us, Robin?'

Somebody sniggered.

'I'm not a teacher,' Robin said. 'I wouldn't presume to be one.'

Silence fell but nobody made a move – the feeling seemed to be that the business of the evening was unfinished.

Hubert Greenstock rose to his feet and cleared his throat.

'My name is Greenstock and I am Robin's vicar,' he began. 'I have counselled innumerable parishioners who had received aerial advice, and I trust I shall not commit sacrilege by endorsing one of Robin's opinions, to wit that the vocalists in general appear to have a robust sense of humour. But, of course, the most holy exceptions prove the rule I have been stating. The Almighty has communicated by word of mouth to sainted members of our species from Adam onwards. Again, I would agree with Robin that his own experiences could safely be listed under the heading of "auto-suggestion". May I thank him on behalf of everyone here for an interesting talk?'

Two men gave tongue from the back row of chairs, one urging, 'Sit down, old boy,' and the other inquiring, 'What do you think of your vicar, Mr Antrobus?'

Robin did not respond.

A lady, also at the back, asked: 'What's been the effect on you of hearing the voice?'

He replied: 'It's made me ill, but I suppose

148

it's foolhardy of me, as well as ungrateful, to say so.'

Scram interjected: 'Unwell, please, Robin – not ill, thank goodness.'

Robin signified agreement with his doctor.

Another lady said: 'Mr Antrobus, I would like you to know that I've had a perfectly thrilling evening. To think that we have you living in our midst, a man who could have been chosen by God to lead a crusade against modern immorality and cultural decline, has restored my faith to a considerable extent. So far as I'm concerned, you have succeeded where the churches have failed.'

Wendy Paddle spoke.

She said: 'I believe it was God,' and was hushed and scolded by the older Patels.

Max now ran true to type by announcing anti-climactically that decent white wine and nibbles were on offer in the kitchen.

Before anyone could react, Father Murphy asked a second question: 'Aren't you honour bound to teach us something, Robin?'

Robin had a question of his own: 'Am I?'

'Well, aren't you? You've been commanded to teach the people, that's us. What's it to be?'

'I don't know.'

'God has no patience with the don't-knows. Surely you know that, Robin?'

'All I know is that I should go home, Father.'

'No, no – you've challenged the Scribes and Pharisees, Robin, namely the Reverend Hubert and myself – you can't run away when we challenge you.'

149

'I never meant to challenge anyone.'

'What? You've thrown mud in our faces, as we say in Ireland. You've said you had the hot line to God Almighty. Now you say you're going to disregard the commandment of God. A good teacher you are, teaching us not to obey the orders of our Holy Father!'

'It's not like that, honestly!'

'Prove me wrong, please, if you're the honest one!'

'Oh Father!'

'No excuses! By all the rules, you're ratting. I'm sorry I have to say that you're a coward, Robin.'

Max spoke up.

'Listen, can't we get on to the wine and nibbles?'

Zinnia said in an audible undertone to Robin: 'You'll have to answer. You can't allow yourself to be called a coward.'

'But I am one,' Robin replied in a thick voice that quavered.

'Don't cry! I forbid you! Be a man!'

There was an awkward silence.

Robin sat on his chair, his face changing colour in a noticeable and even alarming manner. He was wan, then blushing, he closed his eyes, and seemed to be worse than unwell.

But he managed to get on his feet.

'Against my will...' he started and stopped. 'Against my will and my character...' He restarted, and, summoning a smile, said with increasing fluency: 'I hate controversy, I hate arguing, but... But I must admit that my researches for my book, and the book they were meant to become, do amount to a critique of religions. My criticism, my lesson if you like, is twofold. First, racial differences inevitably give rise to different religions; but it's a mistake, it's stupid, that the different religions should then breed like rabbits. Jesus expected Christianity to be assimilated by Judaism: St Paul had other ideas. Christianity based itself in Rome: Martin Luther, Henry the Eighth, John Wesley, and all the other forceful and rebellious persons contributed to the total of the 22,000 Anglican sects. In short, God is scarcely recognisable because he has too many faces. Secondly, the blood lust of religions is a great sin. Christianity has been as bloodthirsty as those who crucified its founder. Many religions are no better, some are worse. I've been asked hard questions. The question I'm sure – yes, I am sure – God would like *me* to ask is when are the religious institutions going to get their act together, and when will they renounce savagery?'

Strong applause greeted this statement. Everyone stood up. A crowd encircled Robin, congratulating him, patting him, kissing him and shaking his hand. Hubert Greenstock and Dylan Murphy slipped away. Max sang out from the kitchen doorway: 'Come to the cookhouse, boys!' The Padger sisters approached Robin.

Rhoda said to him in a conspiratorial undertone: 'We're so very glad you hit those Roman Catholics for six. Good night and thank you.'

Before he could answer that he had intended nothing of that sort, the heavy hand of Bill Rickitt slapped him on the back.

'Mr Antrobus,' Bill said in a loud voice, 'you've explained to me why I don't go to church. Ta for that. See you!'

Zinnia was already introducing two youngish men to Robin, and filling his cup of bitter regrets to the brim.

She said: 'Bill Tilyard's the editor of the *Boroughfare Gazette*, and Mike Wiggs writes for *The Argus*.'

11

Robin was shattered. He had been distracted by the thumping of his heart throughout his talk, and the effects of the unwise things he had said convinced him that he would collapse at any minute. But somehow he survived the wine and nibbles interlude, and, having shaken the last hand and said the last goodnight, he slumped on to Zinnia's sofa.

His cousins returned from seeing the guests off, and Zinnia asked him: What's the matter with you?'

'I feel awful,' he replied.

'Ill?'

'Yes – and I've made such a fool of myself.'

Max asked: 'Are you going to be sick?'

'Oh Max!'

Zinnia said: 'I thought you spoke well – and as you know I don't often pay you compliments. Robin did well, Max, didn't he?'

'I second that – quite a performance – although he's stirred up trouble for us by tweaking our Father Murphy's nose.'

'But it was my nose that was tweaked,' Robin protested.

'Poor Dylan,' Zinnia remarked, 'you beat him up good and proper.'

'That's an exaggeration. And I was provoked, Dylan provoked me, you provoked me, and you and Max together provoked me into getting on my hind legs and spouting a lot of rot.'

'I thought God was the provocative one – He told you to teach everybody,' Max said.

Zinnia played the peacemaker.

'Don't worry, Robin. You really were good – and brave, considering your health.'

'Oh well – thanks for organising the evening – I'd better be going home.'

'Shouldn't Max walk you home?'

'Certainly not – I can manage – but I need my hat and coat.'

'And your stick,' Max said.

'Yes, my stick too, thank you.'

He struggled into the British Warm, and on the way out inquired: 'Why were the journalists here?'

Zinnia said: 'We thought they'd be interested,' and Max growled ominously: 'They were.'

Robin tottered home. He had not kissed Zinnia goodbye. He did not love her this evening, and he hated Max, as usual. He was not in a fit state to be walking anywhere in the night, but preferred to face his fate alone rather than have Max sniping at him.

He reached The Nest, locked his front door, ate some cereal and a mouse's portion of cheese, drank a glass of milk, and retired to bed.

Sleep eluded him. He thought of what he should not have said. His prayers did not pacify him for a long time – he was upset by his cousins' mischief and even by God, who had cast him into the snakepit of his problems.

The morning after was at least a little different: he could not wake up. Eventually consciousness smote him and condensed itself into anxiety. His heart reminded him that it could be compared to the hangman's trapdoor. He had been buffeted by shocks, and, he recollected, shock could well be the death of him with or without assistance of the cardiac kind.

He was bed-bound for most of the day. Immobility seemed to be one way not to irritate his heart. At the same time he recalled the contrarian theory of modern medicine that the heart should be strengthened by running up and down stairs. There was seldom a 'right' course of action, despite Buddhism's assertion that 'rightness' opens the door to nirvana, as Robin noted by force of habit for use in his superseded book.

He thought of trying to discuss everything with Scram; but Scram, whose powers of concentration on his patients' health was notoriously limited, would only want to talk about Robin's talk. He thought of Dr Walker, but remembered that he was waiting for Dr Walker's diagnosis and prognosis, and mentally zapped to another programme.

He dwelt upon, and worried over, two interpretations of recent events. One was that he had been granted the strength to speak in public by transcendental means. He might have died of doing so but for the grace of God. Alternatively,

God had not spoken to him, took no interest in him, had let him publicise his weird fancies and embarrass himself for ever.

A worse scenario he shied away from: that somebody up there or down below had decided to drive him to his doom.

Luckily he had food in the house. He ate it, dozed, watched TV. He watched TV for children, for cooks, for news featuring politicians and crooks, and was back in bed at an early hour, praying to be delivered from evil.

Friday morning did not start well. He noticed that he had been hearing nothing from his neighbours. He was afraid that he had inhibited them with his boast of being closely related to God. No singing in the bath, no rude noises, came through the party wall he shared with the Rickitts, and the Padger sisters moved their furniture with discretion. He wished he had not given them other wrong ideas, that he was anti-church, especially the Church of Rome.

Then, as he ate breakfast, the telephone rang.

It was Max, sounding excited.

He said: 'You're in *The Gazette.*'

Robin requested clarification.

'You've made it into *The Gazette* – congratulations!'

'Oh dear!'

'You're on the front page, you're the banner headline – and they've dug up a snapshot of you taken years ago – they've stuck a mortarboard on your head to make you look like a teacher.'

'What does it say?'

'Here's the headline, "Chimp in the Kremlin".'

'What's that about?'

'I'll read you the first paragraph. "Robin Antrobus of The Nest, Roebuck Road, has claimed in a speech that a chimpanzee would have governed Russia better than Lenin."'

'I never claimed such a thing.'

'You did. I heard you with my own ears. I thought it was a good joke. But Bill Tilyard – he's the editor – he's done his bit of stirring. The old commies aren't going to like to read that Lenin wasn't as clever as a chimp.'

'Oh dear oh dear!'

'Do you want to see the paper?'

'No.'

'Don't take it the wrong way, Robin! You're getting publicity. Isn't publicity what you'd want for your book, if or when it's done?'

'I hate publicity.'

'You are a rum cove. I expected you to be pleased.'

They rang off.

Robin changed his mind. He finished his breakfast, and curiosity combined with a pang or two of excitement chased him out of the house and into Coronation Street on his way to the Patels' newsagency.

An unknown stranger, female, elderly, lady-like, detained him.

'Mr Antrobus?'

'Yes?'

'Your speech was wonderful the other night.'

'Really?'

He could not help glowing a little. Nobody had praised him quite like that before.

'I join you wholeheartedly in disapproving of religion.'

'I didn't mean any such thing – you've misunderstood, Madam.'

'Goodbye,' she said, undeterred and smiling sweetly.

She must have been deaf. She had put her own words into his mouth that he had opened too wide at Zinnia's do. His spirits sank as fast as they had risen. He proceeded to his destination.

Jayendra, standing behind his counter, greeted him thus: 'Oh, Mr Antrobus, we listened to your speech.' He had to stop and serve a customer who was buying a basketful of goods. Robin was disappointed by the interruption and the lack of a word of appreciation – 'listened' was not 'enjoyed' – and sad to be branded a speechmaker. Other shoppers queued at the checkout, partly to stare at him, he suspected. Jayendra was finally free to resume: 'Yes, I was saying – so sorry – that we listened and were interested. Indira was very pleased to be listening to you. Your cousins were good to invite us. But, Mr Antrobus, there were newspaper persons present, and you called Islam political.'

Again, shoppers interrupted, and now Robin waited apprehensively as well as impatiently.

At length he was able to ask: 'Have I dropped a brick, Jayendra?'

'You will take care, sir – take good care.'

'Yes, yes – thank you – I only came in for a *Gazette*.'

Jayendra indicated the newspaper shelf, Robin bought his paper, carried it home folded and hidden under his arm, opened it in his workroom and read the story on the front page.

The explanation of its first paragraph was that Lenin and Stalin were mass murderers and chimps only killed one another occasionally and in order to eat meat.

Its second paragraph ran: 'Mr Antrobus, a historian, also put two fingers up at churches in general and the Church of England in particular. He said the New English Bible read like Whitehall gobbledygook. He wanted all the Protestant congregations to cave in to the Vatican. He accused organised religion of sanctioning bloody sacrifices. Robin Antrobus is the author of a slim volume, *Let's Wallop God*, published in the 1960s, and believes he has heard voices from outer space.'

He was appalled. His heart was missing beats. He had to sit down in his armchair. Time passed. The day began to pass. His initial reaction was modified – he would not immediately jump to his death from Westminster Bridge. Later in the morning he made up his mind to go and buy food at Tesco's. Luckily it was drizzling – he could pull down the brim of his porkpie and shelter under his umbrella.

In the afternoon his telephone rang again. He let it ring twenty times before he caved in and lifted the receiver.

It was Zinnia, and she was saying: 'You see, you're famous.'

'Oh – Zinnia...'

'I told you that if you followed instructions – I mean by teaching – you'd get somewhere for a change, and look what's happened already!'

'If you're referring to *The Gazette*, I resent it, I'm horrified, and I can't help blaming you for inviting Bill Tilyard to the talk.'

'I'm referring to *The Argus*, too.'

'What?'

'Mike Wiggs has done a piece on you.'

'Did you know he was going to, Zinnia?'

'I did not. And don't you be narky with me! It's high time for you to make a mark on the world, Robin.'

'What does *The Argus* say?'

'Shall I read it to you?'

'Go on!'

' "Robin Antrobus of The Nest, Roebuck Road, says he has a direct line to God Almighty. He divulged his secret in a private talk to an audience of getting on for fifty. The venue was the flat in Coronation Street of his cousin, Ms Zinnia Jones. Mr Antrobus, a sometime historian and by all accounts a shy individual, came out of his shell with a vengeance last Wednesday evening. He said he was God's heir, that he had been told he was due to inherit the Kingdom of Heaven. He also said he had been appointed by the Governor of Governors to teach the world its ABC. He again made his first class sit up and take notice by casting aspersions on Christians and communists. Look out, Robin – if you're not careful somebody's going to turn your breast red, blood red." '

'Thanks a lot,' Robin said.

'What's wrong now?' Zinnia retorted.

'You're responsible, you and Max.'

'Do you mean for the journalists? I only tipped them the wink.'

'You shouldn't have.'

'I'm not letting you go to the dogs, Robin. God seems to be thinking as I do. We both want to cheer you up and cheer you on. I don't know if it really is God speaking to you, but, if it is God for some unknown reason, I do believe He wouldn't want you to keep Him all to yourself. Don't worry about public opinion! Your talk was quite good. There!'

'Oh well! I am appreciative, but my life's turned upside down. I wish I'd been struck dumb in the Rec ten days ago. Luckily my heart's going to be the death of me.'

'Have you heard from the specialist?'

'Not yet.'

'You weren't ill after your talk?'

'No – not yet.'

'My advice is, eat, drink and be merrier. Here's another "not yet" for you – you're not expected upstairs at once. Think on these things, as somebody else could well say.'

They giggled – their family talent for seeing the funny side had saved many a day for them.

Robin mentioned Ab's Caf on Sunday evening, would she like to make it a threesome again?

She said yes, adding: 'I'll share the damage with you.'

'But you paid for the wine and nibbles on Wednesday. It's my shout.'

'Are you still afloat financially?'

'I'm hoping the Almighty's keeping an eye on my money.'

They giggled again and said goodbye.

Robin stood by the telephone in his hall. He was dithering. In his own terminology, he felt 'churned up'. He had offended people, bagged the limelight by accident, been betrayed, been misrepresented, was threatened by celebrity, and did not know where to turn or what to turn for. On impulse, almost involuntarily, perhaps in hopes of mending one of the fences he had broken, he looked in his list of useful telephone numbers and rang Hubert Greenstock.

'I'm afraid it's Robin Antrobus,' he said in a strangulated voice.

'Good evening, Robin.'

'Oh – is it evening already? Am I bothering you?'

'No – not at all – I was hoping to speak to you.'

'Really? Oh dear! I was afraid of that.'

'You sound worried, Robin. Could I help?'

Robin was still more bewildered. He had been braced to have his head bitten off.

'Can I come and see you?' he asked.

'Tonight?' Hubert said.

'Tonight – oh! It's not terrifically urgent, but tonight would be wonderful.'

'Shall we say six-o'clock? I can offer you a glass of our homemade white wine. Dorothea and I dine at seven.'

Robin said: 'Until then,' and squirmed a little

– he and Hubert were not close, and he was nonplussed by the vicar's transformation and suspected an ulterior motive.

At the appointed hour, having walked to the vicarage without being accosted or assaulted, he rang the doorbell of St Columb's vicarage.

Hubert opened the door and shook Robin's hand between both of his.

In the study he poured liquid from a bottle into two small glasses: it was more brown than white. He presented one glass to Robin, they raised their glasses to each other, and sat down as before, on either side of the electric fire, one bar aglow.

Robin had to cough – the wine was as rough as sandpaper – but finally said: 'I must apologise.'

'Why is that?'

'You might have thought I was disrespectful on Wednesday. *The Gazette* and *The Argus* have printed articles that accuse me of insulting the Church of England.'

'My Church and yours is not beyond reproach,' Hubert admitted, with a smile that mingled sympathy and sanctimoniousness.

'But I didn't mean to insult it or insult anybody,' Robin insisted.

'Your criticisms struck me as constructive, and as such useful.'

'Father Murphy pushed me further than I meant to go.'

'You are not alone, Robin, in having been brainwashed by one of Father Murphy's inquisitions.'

'He's always been nice to me – we know each other through my cousins who are Catholics – and Mrs Connolly and I meet in the aisles of Tesco. Father Murphy was nice when I consulted him about my voices.'

'Ah!'

'I probably owe you another apology for consulting him after consulting yourself.'

'How "nice" was he, may I ask?'

'Well – it's very comfortable in The Priest's House – and I had a delicious tea there.'

'He would have been less sceptical than I had been, no doubt. Irish people are apt to be credulous.'

'My cousins made me consult him.'

'I see.'

'Mrs Connolly kissed my hand.'

'She is an excitable and demonstrative woman.'

'I suppose so.'

'She knew about the voice?'

'Father Murphy told her.'

'She would have regarded you as a candidate for canonisation. I personally think it would be premature to grant you sainthood.'

Robin laughed at the preposterousness of the idea.

'On the other hand, the Church of Rome is a law unto itself.'

Robin laughed again, but uneasily: had Hubert cracked a joke?

Hubert looked hard at Robin through his specs and inquired: 'Are you acquainted with the countryside and its metaphors?'

Robin had to request clarification.

Hubert explained: 'My father was a countryman. He enjoyed country sports. I took a decision after your talk at Zinnia's house. I decided that I couldn't allow Dylan Murphy to kill my fox. Do you understand, Robin?'

'No, actually.'

'You and I would both be wrong to let Roman Catholicism make off with the prize won by a Protestant for Protestantism,' Hubert said with a mixture of aplomb and smugness.

'Heavens!'

'I beg your pardon?'

'Sorry – I just hadn't thought of anything like that.'

Hubert came near to enthusing: 'Considerable kudos would accrue to the religion with a communicant who had been honoured by the receipt of messages from our Blessed Lord. Surely that's crystal clear, Robin. Our Church is neither grasping nor selfish, but it would not like to let a golden opportunity slip through its fingers and into the arms of the Pope. Why should the Vatican have all the saints?'

'Hubert, I really feel...'

'I'm sorry to say that your personal feelings will be of small account from now on. You have gone public, as they say; and I would submit that your Church has every right to represent you in your dealings with its Founder. You have apologised to me, and it's my turn to apologise. A single message resembles the single swallow that does not make a summer. Two messages

165

have convinced me that I could have failed you with my scepticism. I am not of a mind to kiss your hand, Robin, but I am convinced that you have reported honestly and, from a religious viewpoint, I may be looking at my superior.'

'Hubert – please – I must leave you.'

'So soon? You have not drunk your wine.'

'I'm half a teetotaller – thanks all the same.'

'I'll fetch your coat, Robin.'

'Oh, thank you. It's a British Warm.'

'I had not heard of that type of overcoat before.'

'It's army, it belonged to my father, not the holy one,' he giggled foolishly, owing to stress.

A shadow crossed Hubert's face, but he shook Robin's hand and said: 'God bless you.'

'Thanks again,' Robin returned. 'Love to Dorothea,' he tacked on, although he scarcely knew her.

In Coronation Street he inhaled deep breaths of North London air. He was relieved to be out of Hubert Greenstock's competitive clutches. But his relief was merging with mournfulness. He had been more than misunderstood by everyone. He had produced effects that were the exact opposite of the causes he embraced. His constructivism was destructive. He was almost like one of those poor people who say the opposite of what they are trying to say.

He approached The Nest, apologising finally in his head and heart to his Maker. He saw white on his black front door, large white letters painted on it, then read two words, one above the other: 'CLASS ENMY'.

It was communist – an illiterate commie had done it – Robin was targeted for telling the truth about Lenin – and he was frightened, he feared he would be beaten by louts inside his home, and hesitated in the roadway.

He was called by name by a girl on the opposite pavement: she was Wendy Paddle.

'Hi, Mr Antrobus, sir!'

'Oh Wendy, look at what they've done!'

He pointed at his door. She read and groaned.

'How bad!' she exclaimed.

'I don't know if they're in my house – they may be waiting for me.'

'Will I look in, sir?'

'No, you can't do that, you mustn't.'

'Sir, I am not so valuable as you are.'

'Oh Wendy,' he repeated in a thicker voice, and then said: 'Would you be very kind and stay out here, well away from my house, while I go in? If all's well, I'll let you know.'

'Please, sir, yes.'

He thanked her. He went and opened his door. He checked the ground floor and hurried upstairs. He descended the stairs, crossed the road, and spoke to Wendy.

'Thank you so much. You've made everything better. But I'm not valuable, Wendy. Good night.'

'Good night, Mr Antrobus.'

He went back into the house, locked his door, and leant his forehead against it.

12

In fact, everything was worse.

On Saturday Robin sought advice from the DIY shop in Boroughfare, bought paint-stripper, paint and paint brushes, and set to work on his front door. Bill Rickitt, driving by in his juggernaut, stopped, found out what Robin was up to and why, and said he would set the local fascists on to the commies. Disregarding pleas for tolerance and peace, Bill said: 'Those Nazis won't half knock the reds about for you, Mr Antrobus, believe you me!' Then Ruth Padger, Robin's neighbour and the gentler of the Padger sisters, reacted to his story by whispering that she would like communists to be torn limb from limb. Marge Rickitt returned heavy-laden with Tesco bags and uttered some swear-words sympathetically. Other women, after he had removed the white paint, suggested that it had not needed doing. Other men took the trouble to tell him he had done the job wrong.

He did not finish until late afternoon, was displeased by his runs and blobs of paint, also exhausted, and Wendy Paddle rang his doorbell. A bespectacled youth growing a black beard stood behind her.

'I hope we are not disturbing you, sir,' Wendy said.

Robin fibbed in the negative.

'You have painted your door. We would have painted it for you.'

'Thank you, but...'

'I see. So sorry! Mr Antrobus, this is John.'

She pointed at the youth, and Robin guessed he was her suitor – formerly, Jehan.

She confirmed it.

'He is half an Englishman now, Mr Antrobus. He has changed his name, and we may both be changing our religion.'

'I hope not because of me, Wendy. I fear your father is cross with me – he thinks I've influenced you to reject your family traditions.'

'He is not right. Islam is for men, but I am telling John to grow up and be modern. You are not to blame, sir.'

'I'd rather not offend the Muslim authorities as well as the communists.'

'We will protect you, Mr Antrobus. We wished to say that we will pass this way and try to prevent harm to your property.'

'That's a kind thought.'

'All will be well, sir.'

'Will it?'

'Of course!'

They said goodbye.

Night fell, and next day, in the dawn, Robin sallied forth to the Communion Service at St Columb's.

It was embarrassing. He had to run the gauntlet

first of the worshippers leaving for St Mary's, some of whom were evidently aware of his possible inheritance. They cast glances at him that ranged from respectful to jaundiced – jaundiced because he was going to the other church. Then the worshippers at St Columb's, who were equally well-informed, smiled and nodded at him approvingly because he was not a Roman Catholic, and stood aside to let him get to the altar rail before anyone else.

Luckily Hubert Greenstock did not draw attention to Robin. He interrupted the service alarmingly after the Collect, but it was only to read a long list of the sick and disabled. Robin escaped almost in the act of being blessed, scuttled home, and stayed put until his cousins arrived in the evening.

They walked to Ab's Caf and occupied their usual table. They ordered their usual food and drink. But Robin had unusual news for them: that he was a 'class enmy' and a so-called legitimate target for bolshies; that he might have a lethal Muslim fatwa slapped on him; that his vicar was fashioning him into a stick with which to belabour Roman Catholics; that almost everything he had talked about in Zinnia's flat had been edited by members of the audience in such a way as to give it an opposite meaning; and, in short, he was near the end of his tether. Zinnia and Max were not so responsive as he had hoped they would be. They munched their fodder and appeared to be bored. Zinnia did ask if God had wagged his tongue again, and Max wanted

170

to know if the press had been in touch; but otherwise they both seemed to have other things on their minds. Halfway through the escalopes Zinnia prompted Max, who laid down his knife and fork and cleared his throat.

'My finances have taken a turn for the south,' he said.

Robin waited.

'I'm in the red pretty deep.'

'Not again?' Robin asked rhetorically.

No one answered.

'The company doctor should heal himself,' Robin quipped.

'Not funny, old boy,' Max growled.

'What's the damage?'

'It's in grands.'

'How many?'

'Two – two and a bit.'

'How were you able to run up such a bill?'

'Credit cards, store cards, and interest on the overdrafts. I had to equip my flat – it had to look as if the company doctor was doing well.'

'How are you going to pay?'

'You've hit the button.'

Zinnia intervened.

She addressed Robin: 'We'll have to mount another rescue operation.'

He demanded details, and listened to a plan to hire a big hall in which he – Robin – would spout religion at fifty quid a ticket. The escalopes were eaten and replaced by ice creams and the Peach Melba – Max had not thought of economising for the sake of his host. At length, over coffee and cream, Max had the grace to say he was sorry.

'Trouble is I've had rotten luck ever since I volunteered to join the army, and worse luck since I was invalided out. God hasn't given me the sort of boost He's given you, Robin. God in his wisdom's turned me into His whipping boy.'

Robin said he would have to think things over: he was refusing to be rushed into ruining himself.

Max said: 'I don't want to go bankrupt. I couldn't sign a cheque if they bankrupted me.'

'You shouldn't be signing cheques anyway. But nobody's going to pay to bankrupt you. The people you owe money to will just give your name to strong-arm debt collectors.'

Zinnia told Robin not to be unkind to Max, Max said he was not and never had been scared of little old Robin, and Robin said they had better go home before there was more unpleasantness.

The next morning brought Robin a letter coincidentally connected with the previous evening. It was from Lindsey Addiscombe, his solicitor, senior partner at Addiscombe and Lea, who looked after his financial affairs, just as Douglas Addiscombe, Lindsey's father, had done for his parents. A company had gone bust, Lindsey wrote, Robin held shares in it which were now worthless, the capital and the income of his portfolio were therefore affected, and a meeting in the near future would be advisable.

Robin knew nothing about money. That is, he had always had just enough to pay for his way of life, yet had feared penury from the day his father died. His mother was left an adequate jointure; he had not been forgotten by his father; and when he was orphaned he inherited what Lindsey called 'a sizeable sum'. He was nonetheless aware of his dependence on the status quo. He panicked every year before the Budget, during it, and afterwards, until he was reassured by Lindsey. He had nightmares in which he was evicted from The Nest. He saw himself selling matches. His constitution and his nervous system did not equip him to be poor.

He rang Lindsey and fixed an appointment for that Monday afternoon. After lunch he caught the bus to North Boroughfare and arrived at the premises of Addiscombe and Lea an hour before his appointment. Would his heart withstand the interview? It had been sorely tested ever since he read that wretched letter.

At last Lindsey emerged from his office and conducted Robin to the chair on the clients' side of the desk – it might as well have been electric.

The news was not terrible, Lindsey said. He was Robin's age, and had experience of the timid Antrobus temperament. He smiled benevolently and said Robin had lost no more than five thousand pounds, which had yielded a dividend that would scarcely be missed. Robin heard himself agreeing that everything in his garden was very nearly as rosy as ever. The question of recovering the five thousand was neither raised nor answered.

Lindsey was more eager to ask than to answer questions. He broached the subject of the articles in *The Gazette* and *The Argus*. It was Robin's turn to be impatient. The journalists had obeyed the first rule of journalism and misreported him. The story of the voices he had heard was grossly exaggerated, he insisted.

In the bus homeward bound he estimated the number of coach tours, train journeys, cruises and flights to romantic destinations he could have bought for five thousand pounds. He did not know how much he was worth altogether – his preference had always been not to know how much richer he was than his cousins and the poor people. Whatever the total was, it was five thousand less than it had been, and he was definitely not going to pauperise himself by propping up Max's finances.

But to take a decision in principle is easier than to act upon it. Throughout the remainder of Monday Robin wriggled on the sharp end of the prospect of having to say nothing doing to Max. He would be scourged by the knotted tongue of Zinnia. He would be accused of minginess and selfishness, and, above all, of being unworthy of the interest that the powers-that-be had apparently taken in him. Again, God was complicating the issue: as a result of His interference, a financial disagreement between friends was about to be dragged into the courts where sinners are judged.

Tuesday dawned. Tuesday was a mixed bag of what was better than good and then bad. He received another telephone call. This time it was a foreign woman on the line. She was American, a Texan maybe, but rang from an office in London. She represented a magazine called *Beyond*. She was surprised that Robin had never heard of it, since it was big in America and globally. Its speciality was whatever was beyond reason, logic, knowledge, human intelligence, earth, the solar system and the universe. Robin apologised for his ignorance. She pardoned him and informed him that her name was Suejoe. She was intrigued by 'voices': 'I just love a mystery,' she confessed. She was set on having an account of 'his' voices for *Beyond*. She wanted it while it was 'hot' and would pay seven thousand five hundred pounds.

He gasped.

'You're a writer, Robin – write the piece for us,' Suejoe urged. 'You could speak it – or even get it written for you. We reserve the right to edit all material. May I send you a contract?'

Robin said no. He arrived at the negative by a roundabout route. He was rendered almost speechless by the offer to start with. Eventually he agreed to ring Suejoe back in a day or two.

Beyond would solve one problem: it would replenish his coffer. And Suejoe made a long or short article by himself, descriptive of the mystery of the voices and drawing his own individualistic conclusions, sound simple: she summed it up as money for jam. Little did she know! He could write nothing that would spare him irrefutable charges of letting down, exposing, ungratefully sneering at, and selling God all over again for filthy lucre.

He quailed already in case his cousins should discover that he had been handed a not so small fortune on a plate and had rejected it. He would be called mad at best, and at worst an egocentric swine. But if he had accepted the offer, he would have felt guilty about taking the money, guilty about hiding it, and furious if he were forced by his cousins to disgorge it.

He pleaded his case to himself repeatedly. *Beyond* was not in the business of keeping the secrets of its contributors. People would read his article, should he write it. Church people would pass it on to Hubert Greenstock and Dylan Murphy. Zinnia and Max would be informed, and he would get it in the neck. He would be investigated by all and sundry, and severely punished at least by international publicity.

Suejoe had seemed to be an angel despatched from above, from beyond indeed, to help him; and was revealed as a temptress. He had been right to resist her blandishments, but suffered from doing so.

On the next day, Wednesday, he had three more reasons to question the goodness of God.

He received notification of an appointment with Dr Walker at Southwood Hospital on the Friday afternoon. The results of his blood test must have come through, and his pessimism was in the ascendant.

Secondly, later in the morning, an uninvited visitor rang his doorbell. Mrs Connolly stood before him, wreathed in smiles and bedecked in

176

brightly coloured raiment. She asked if she could pop in for a word in his ear.

He ushered her into the kitchen. When he explained that there was really nowhere to sit in his front room, she said: 'That's where it's all gestating.' He was not pleased by her choice of words, and could not decide whether or not to offer her a cup of tea.

'I hope I'm not interrupting the act of creation,' she said, and again he found private fault with her seminal imagery. 'I'm here with a proposition,' she added with what looked like a conspiratorial smirk.

Robin offered her a chair by way of compromise.

'No, my dear man,' she replied, 'and don't tantalise me! I'm only here for my Father.' It was a joke – she meant her employer. 'He's wanting you for lunch.' This was also jocular. 'I'll give you my Irish stew and soda bread, and Guinness, and I tell you, good sir, because I know gentlemen through and through, that yourself and Father Dylan and the Lord God Above will be thick as thieves before the meal's half-done. Next week it is, any day midweek, and I'm not taking no for an answer.'

But she had to take it. He told her he was seeing his cardiac specialist on the coming Friday, and could make no plans for the future.

She comforted, patted, petted and ended by hugging him, and as she went out she made the ominous promise that Father Murphy would be praying for his survival.

Robin mooned round his house. Work was

out of the question. He did not know what to do with himself. He had lunch early, at noon or thereabouts. His doorbell rang again while he was eating. He let it ring a second time, and lengthily, before he felt he must open the door.

Three men were on his doorstep, strangers more or less bearded. They did not wait to be invited in, they strode past him, brushed past, unsmiling, and the boss man ordered, 'Shut the door!'

He was short and portly, and had the hairiest head Robin had ever seen. His hair was inky black with a crinkle, sprouted from his scalp in every direction and formed hedge-like eyebrows. His moustache and beard began under his eyes and ended at nipple-height. His eyeballs were buried in the thicket of his hair, but occasionally a glimmer of white peeped through. He said in a cockney voice almost as surprising as his appearance: 'We're Muslims from the Mosque – I'm the Imam.'

'Oh yes?' Robin queried with an incorrigible quaver.

'We don't need a lot of your time, just enough to put things straight,' the Imam explained. 'The word is you've been getting messages. If they're genuine, bully for you. If there's no fiddling about, we'll roll the red carpet. Time will tell. But we've come along to warn you not to bad-mouth our religion.'

'I haven't.'

'We're kept informed, mate.'

'I haven't spoken ill of the Founder or foundations of Islam.'

'We don't like blasphemers.'

'I'm well aware of that, and have spoken nothing but the truth. Your religion respects the truth.'

'Mr Antrobus, you know what's what. Our religion's stricter than yours. We guard our good name and our faithful people. We don't play games.'

'I quite understand.'

'That's lucky then. Good day to you.'

A tooth glinted through his hairiness, Robin was being smiled at, and one of the two acolytes opened his front door. The Imam was stepping out, but Robin detained the other two, young black men with muscles but beards that were more like tufts.

'Excuse me,' he said to them. 'Don't I know you? Didn't you help me up one evening when I tripped and fell in the road?'

The boys looked sheepish, then at one another. One murmured, 'Yah.'

The Imam intervened: 'We're for mercy and compassion, Mr Antrobus. That's our message – please to remember it.'

'Oh I will – thank you – goodbye!'

They left the house. Robin made sure the door was closed. His heart was more frightening than his visitors had been. It seemed to be trying to jump out of his mouth. He slowly mounted the stairs and lay down on his bed.

The rest of Wednesday was a blank. He sucked his white pills and waited for his heart to settle: it did, before he thought he ought to summon an ambulance. His mental meanderings took a self-preservative turn. He dredged up un-contaminated memories of his mother, and of her pride in him and confidence that he was going to win. He remembered the contentment amounting to happiness of the even tenor of the years before God had seen fit to interfere. He tried not to think of Max, money, *Beyond*, and especially Wendy Paddle, an unfaithful Muslim, a possible or actual Muslim apostate, whom he had not sent packing back to her parents and her religious guardians, who might not be merciful in his case. He had tea, then dinner, watched TV and returned to his bed.

Thursday was exceptional. It was a sort of day off for Robin. He kept his worries at bay. He lived for pleasure, went to Tesco's in the morning, and in the afternoon took a bus ride to and from the West End of London.

On Friday morning Robin was sure he was not well enough to see the doctor. He had slept badly. He would have rung Zinnia if she had not always suspected he was a coward. He would have rung Max if he had not been sure that he would only be told how many tests Max had undergone. Loneliness had been his lot, he had settled for it, perhaps chosen it, but today he was overwhelmed with regrets.

He dressed with care – white shirt, tie, suit and black shoes – as if he were going to a wedding, or, it occurred to him, a funeral. He found a little comfort in his British Warm and hid from prying eyes under his pork-pie. He hurried towards Boroughfare station across the Recreation Ground.

He caught a train and arrived at Southwood Hospital two hours before his appointment.

At length Robin was summoned into the consulting room, and sat on one side of the desk while Dr Walker sat on the other, studying notes and reports.

The verdict was sickening. There were irregularities and warning signs. More tests were essential, a scan, an angiogram. The possibility of a future infarction could not be ruled out. At some stage a bypass or two would be advisable.

Robin's heart reacted badly to Dr Walker's diagnosis. It began to flutter. Dr Walker called for a nurse to escort Robin elsewhere and watch over him. Robin was led away by the hand, into an empty recovery room with makeshift beds to lie on. His British Warm, pork-pie, and the jacket of his suit were removed, and his tie loosened. He asked if he could go to the lavatory, and she led him across to a so-called disabled toilet, spacious enough to allow the manoeuvring of wheelchairs. He was on no account to lock the door.

The flush of the lavatory pan was exceptionally fierce and noisy. As one noise subsided another reverberated. He recognised it. He had heard it twice before. Someone was saying to him, 'Your seat in Paradise is reserved.'

13

Robin thought he was passing over in the disabled toilet, but actually he passed out. The shock of hearing that voice again, of it issuing apparently from the lavatory pan, of the message it had for him, amounting to a summons to hurry up to Paradise, combined with all that had gone before, defeated his constitution.

He came to in Intensive Care. He had suffered a heart attack and concussion caused by falling over and hitting his head on the disabled bidet. He was connected by tubes to bottles; electrodes were stuck all over his torso; an inflatable armband automatically monitored his blood pressure. He was not in pain or noticeably unhappy.

He was reprieved. He was unlikely to die with nurses looking after him on a twenty-four hour basis, and doctors on call. He could postpone decisions, he could stop thinking. He delegated responsibility for his being. It was a sort of holiday.

There were eight patients in the ward, and four nurses at a time were in charge of them. Most of the patients were iller than Robin. Quiet reigned – no TV or radio, and voices hushed as a rule. Routine and discipline were clearly considered to be aids to recovery. And the food was good. After the strangeness of Robin's where-abouts had worn off he had to admit he was having a nice time.

He was not allowed visitors for thirty-six hours. Somebody had contacted Zinnia on his behalf, but life without cousins also contributed to his holiday mood. Unfortunately, in the forty-first hour Max strode into the ward. He brought a posy of flowers; it was immediately confiscated as flowers were not permitted, and Max then complained to Robin that they had cost him 'a bomb' and he should have been warned.

An unremedial conversation ensued.

'Bad show, this!'

'I'm okay.'

'You chose the right spot, a hospital, to pull a wobbly.'

'I suppose so.'

'Your arm's black.'

'It's the bruising.'

'When are they going to let you out of here?'

'Soon.'

'Soon! That's the problem.'

Robin recognised Max's tone of voice that heralded complications.

'What problem?' he asked faintly.

'You can't be alone in The Nest.'

'What?'

'I've decided to move in with you.'

'Oh no, Max.'

'I knew you'd kick a bit, but there's no alternative. We can't have you popping off on your ownsome. It may not be for long.'

'What do you mean? Are you saying I won't live long?'

'Of course not. I'm not such a fool as that. You could have another year or two ahead. I meant I'd stay in your house until you're up to living alone.'

'It's out of the question.'

'Look here – for once I'm telling you straight that you're a miser – naturally you'd have to pay me for caring – I'd only expect a carer's wage, not a nurse's – but the very idea of your having to cough up makes you start to squeal, as you always do – you're putting your money before your health.'

'Money never entered my head, you're the one who's always on about money.'

'No, Robin, it's not right to jeer at me for being less well-off than you are.'

'No, Max! I don't jeer at you. I'm not paying you to make a nuisance of yourself in my house. I won't let you get the company doctor out of the hole he's in by false pretences at my expense. I'm not going to argue with you, I can't and won't, and that's definite.'

'Are you feeling sick?'

'Yes, I am.'

'Shall I fetch a basin?'

'No – I'm just sick of you – please leave me be.'

'Hell's bells, Robin! It wasn't cheap to get to Southwood.'

'I'll settle up with you another time.'

'If there is one,' Max said under his breath,

and lumbered away. Twenty-four hours later Zinnia came to see him.

'What happened, Robin?' she demanded without much delay. 'You never told Max.'

'He never asked.'

'Tell me!'

'I heard the voice.'

'Where?'

'Here – in a lavatory here – after I was told I'd have to have a bypass operation on my heart.'

'Oh – how awful! How awful for you! But the bypass might make you strong at long last, even if the prospect gave you a heart attack.'

'No – it wasn't the bypass – it was the message.'

'What did the voice have to say for itself this time?'

'"Your seat in Paradise is reserved".'

'Are you joking?'

'No.'

He had to repeat it, and she laughed and said: 'It makes dying sound like going to a movie. It makes you look a fool, Robin. It's piffle. You didn't invent it, did you?'

'I don't know. I don't know what to think.'

'Well, you'd better buck up and start thinking. Honestly, you'll be a laughing stock if you broadcast the latest. And all the God-crowd will be down on you for mocking the Almighty. Besides, the gullible people who believed that the first two messages came from heaven, they'll want to wring your neck.'

'Don't! But, Zinnia, you must agree the message isn't my style. I'm not such a fool as to imagine

Paradise is watching a show of some description. Consciously or subconsciously I wouldn't say that seats could be reserved there. And if it's not me, who is behind the messages?'

'Stop it, Robin – you've got enough to worry about – forget God, for God's sake!'

'He may have invited me to die.'

'That's morbid.'

'Die and join Him.'

'He can't be so short of company that he has to send you an urgent invitation.'

'It's all such a puzzle. The only thing I know for certain is that I'm not going to have Max paid or unpaid in The Nest.'

'Poor chap, he's so hard up.'

'I've lost money too.'

'Your finances and his aren't comparable.'

'Oh Zinnia, please, I'm tired.'

'Very well, I'll be off. But remember, the time's come for you to sort out God, who ought to desist from working you and others into a frenzy with His flirting.'

Robin hushed her, begged her to keep the secret of the third message, and waved her goodbye with another sigh of relief.

His health improved slightly. Dr Walker made an appointment a fortnight ahead and moved him to a convalescent ward for a week's stay. Robin had a slip of a room to himself and, in the hours he spent there alone at night and in the day, he could not help doing Zinnia's bidding. He himself was sorted out, if temporarily; he had not died; and he toyed with the idea that the life ahead of him should differ from, and be better than, the life he had already lived.

Destructiveness struck him as a move in a constructive direction. *The Analogical Review* toppled over and down in a cloud of dust. He could never go back to it. He saw irreparable mistakes, starting with the title: he had called the book 'analogical' because the word struck an impressive note, but in fact he had never known its exact meaning, and had always feared it would come in for criticism. He now acknowledged that the title was worse than a mistake, it was pretentious.

The range of the book was next on his list. The fact that no other book did what he had tried to do was proof that the task was too extensive for successful literary treatment. An omnibus of the ancient and modern histories of the human race, civilisations, nations, peoples, and their vast variety of religions linked with the various genetic types, would have made Gibbon's *Decline and Fall of the Roman Empire* look like pulp fiction. It would have fitted into no library, it would have weighed too much, and been unreadable.

He had wasted his best years on a chimera; but it was better to be late than never – he had to root out the rot by getting rid of the repository. The future without his book, routine, habits, lifelong hopes, was unknown. It was another mystery, akin to the state of his heart, to his three pieces of news from nowhere, and why he had arrived where he now was.

Religion had led him astray. He felt himself teetering on the edge of a precipice, his feet still on the solid ground of a religious world, but darkness before him and mist beneath. He caught his breath as the danger he was in came home to him. How frightened his mother would have been on his account, and his father, how silent! He could not understand why his heart continued to beat, if unevenly, as he seriously contemplated stepping forward instead of back.

The question was, what was there to go back to? An unnecessary book, its content shallow, its claims erroneous; the embers of his faith in Christianity, and his doubts about religious practice in general; his lonely house and his cousins – empty days, purposeless days, nothing except squabbling with Zinnia and Max, a hackneyed pattern and a threadbare existence. Could he bear much more of the same? Could he afford it?

His lifeline of money might drift beyond his reach. He had realised he was about to lose more than five thousand pounds, for he could not withstand Max's almost pitiful appeals, he could not let Max go under. Zinnia would not help much, she never did, she formed a team with her brother to get at Robin's money – they were like a couple of greyhounds cooperating to turn the hare.

A void now opened behind him. Once noticed, it widened, and was lightless, hopeless. He was isolated on a shrinking mountain top, circum-scribed by perils. He had to obey Zinnia in a hurry, he was forced to take a risk by his cousin,

188

by his imaginary situation and the pending operation on his heart.

He was sent home to The Nest. He had formed a plan and convalesced sufficiently to act on it. He rang Suejoe at *Beyond*.

He told her that he had received a third message from elsewhere. Would she be interested in an article that told the story of his messages and their effects on his personal life and religious faith? She was interested. Would she allow him complete freedom of expression in a contractual sense? She would, she promised.

He set to work before the contract arrived. For two days he was packing his papers relating to *The Analogical Review*, and old reference books dog-eared and falling apart, in black bags ready for the refuse collectors. He removed the plasterer's table and the folding tables that had filled the middle of the workroom, and cleared the mantelpiece and the desk in the window. He pushed his favourite armchair from where it had stood against the back wall to its rightful position beside the fireplace. Then, in surroundings that were almost exactly as they had been when he embarked on the fiasco of his career, he began to write not as before, but fluently.

He recorded his messages and described the circumstances in which they were received.

He continued: 'I should explain that I was baptised and christened, have been a practising Christian for all my sixty years, and engaged in writing about religion for two-thirds of my life. Imagine, therefore, the enormous shock of my experience in the Roebuck Recreation Ground! I thought, I almost had to assume, that I was being addressed by God Almighty. I was amazed, flattered to an indescribable degree, and utterly confused. The second message seemed to me to authenticate the first. God would be bound to wish His chosen disciple on earth today to teach people, and thus follow the example of Jesus Christ. The third message had an opposite consequence: it gave support to all the doubters of the authenticity of the other two.

'I myself was overwhelmed with doubt and disappointment. Common sense would not let me believe God had opted to speak to me in a disabled toilet. I had to admit that the message which seemed to be connected with pulling the plug was unacceptable. Paradise could not be an auditorium, a theatre, a cinema, where, after we were resurrected, we watched shows. Resurrection as entertainment was not a bad idea, but did we all need seats in heaven, and was there difficulty in obtaining one, was there standing room only, were people barred from entering Paradise for logistical reasons, because there was no room for them to sit or stand? Surely the Almighty had better things to do than to act as a high-class ticket tout.

'Doubt is notoriously infectious. Why should I have been told to teach? I was never a teacher. I had no teaching to impart. I was prevailed upon to deliver a short talk, but it got me into trouble and I very much regretted it.

'At last I came round to subjecting the original

message to objective analysis. Again, I had to side with the sceptics, who had pointed out that heaven was unlikely to be a monarchy on a worldly pattern, even an absolute monarchy or autocracy. Jesus said he was the Son of God, he never boasted that he was a crown prince. Two thousand years later why would I be picked to step into the shoes – another pair of the shoes – of God? I had no princely qualifications – people who know me would confirm that I always was, and would remain, one of the humbler class and type of persons.

'The conclusion was inescapable. I had been targeted not by God as my religion thinks of Him, not an all-powerful intelligence capable of creating a world and a universe, but either by a ghost with a twisted sense of humour, or by some human practical joker.

'Unfortunately, or perhaps fortunately, my agnosticism, my negative and don't-know attitude, was not the end of the matter. I was not pleased with God, and inwardly voiced the immemorial reproach of simple-minded disbelievers: why did He let such things, bad things, wars, despotism, cruelty, disease, quarrels, happen? From there, from that point, it seemed to be only a short step to adverse criticism of Christianity.

'I am doing my best to tell and write the truth. I have great respect for the faithful throughout the two millennia since Jesus perished, and I envy my contemporaries who retain their faith. It was against my inclinations and my will that I became an apostate.

191

'But there it is: I could not believe in the central tenet of Christianity. Somebody has said: "It's easy to found a religion, all you have to do is to die and three days later rise from the dead." Clever people even in the year dot knew that the most beautiful of all ideas, enshrined in religions, was the defeat of death. Jesus died on the cross, vanished and was resurrected.

'Realistic explanations of the story whittled away at my lifelong acceptance of its accuracy. Jesus appeared to people after the crucifixion. Perhaps He had not died on the cross. Perhaps He was spirited away from Golgotha and enabled to recover from His wounds. Perhaps all the business in the tomb was not what it was reported to have been. The reappearance of a dead man looking alive, keeping his promise that he could and would survive death, was miraculous, the foundation of a religion, or, much more likely, a conjuring trick.

'Virgin birth figured in pre-Christian religions. It was another notion that supported religion because it was at once wonderful and impossible. Moreover, the modesty of the breeding of Jesus, the claim that the child of a carpenter could be God's Son, was the apotheosis of the ever-popular Cinderella theme. Just as everybody was offered the boon and blessing of a second chance by resurrection, so the poor were glorified by the example of the founder of Christianity. No wonder it caught on!

'I could not give any of it the benefit of my own doubt. Who really wrote, who by himself would have been capable of writing, the Gospels? *The Analogical Review* was rapidly turning into a *Critical Review of Religions*. The crux of the argument in which I was engaged was that "creed" was the greatest of all the man-made causes of human misery. Creeds drive people to disagree and fight their neighbours. Creeds, religions, are too ready to offer absolution for the shedding of blood. Often they call for, impose, bless and sanctify bloodshed. The history of religions that I have studied for thirty-odd years drips with blood and with tears.

'And if readers of the above should comfort themselves by thinking that I write of the savage eras of yore, I have to remind them of Marxism, a pseudo-religion preaching cut-price Christianity – heaven on earth if you kill class enemies – Marxism which murdered millions of people in the twentieth century and is still at it.

'The slate cannot be wiped clean. I would suggest that creeds were the invention of the devil if I believed in devils – my devils are criminals. Grievous it is for me to write that I feel better off not to be a Christian. I was conventional, naïve, lazy, to go where my parents had gone, and fearful not to consider the alternative. The word "beyond" is a kind of kaleidoscope for me – it can form different pictures. "Beyond" used to describe the afterlife, resurrection, to which I looked forward. Beyond could be the place where my messages came from, messages that lifted me out of my rut and have cast me down – some would say into outer darkness. Beyond also means the days ahead of me that could be barren, yet more peaceful than my previous sixty years of wrestling with God. Beyond refers to what is beyond understanding in my story. And I contribute to *Beyond*, the magazine, for the sake of all its readers who have suffered, are suffering, and will suffer directly or indirectly from the gods, from creeds and their political derivatives.'

Robin Antrobus had written legibly by hand, as agreed with Suejoe. He folded his pages and put them in an envelope, addressed the envelope, stuck on stamps but did not seal it.

The time was seven o'clock on the evening of the day before he was due to see Dr Walker. He expected to be told when the operation on his heart would take place. He was quite pleased to have written his apologia for atheism – it was probably his last will and testament.

The doorbell rang. He thought of not opening the door, but the lights were on in his front room and visible through the curtains. The bell rang for longer, and he went into the hall and called through the door.

'Who is it?'

'Mr Antrobus, it is John.'

'John?'

'John Patterson – I was called Jehan, sir.'

'I'm sorry – do I know you?'

'I am the friend of Wendy Paddle.'

'Oh yes.'

Robin unlocked the door and opened it a few inches. The boy with the black eyebrows smiled at him.

'Oh yes,' Robin repeated; 'I remember you.'

'Could I speak with you for two minutes, Mr Antrobus?'

Robin opened the door wide, admitted his visitor, and shut the door.

'I didn't recognise your name,' he said.

'Sir, I have changed it by deed poll. I was Jehan Patel, now I am John Patterson. My father don't like it, but Wendy is pleased. Sir, will you help me to marry her? That is why I am here.'

Robin had to smile, but said he was not a matchmaker and did not want to interfere.

'Oh, sir, Wendy believes you. Please – I will explain. We are both English now. My grandfather came to England from India, he was Indian, my father was half Indian and half English, and I am English, like Wendy. But she does not want to be a Muslim woman or wife. She saddens her father, and she is sad, and so am I. Sir, we can be English Muslims – I will not beat my wife, I swear it. Please tell her, Mr Antrobus.'

'I'll do my best if I have a chance, John.'

'Sir, you honour me.'

John shook Robin's hand and bowed over it. Robin spoke.

'Before you go, John, would you do me a favour?'

'Certainly.'

'You are an electronic expert. I have heard voices from somewhere or nowhere, I have heard a voice or voices three times, out of doors, indoors – Wendy heard my talk and probably told you.'

John nodded.

'Would it be possible to "throw" a voice at me electronically, and deliver messages by remote control?'

'I don't think so, Mr Antrobus.'

'Are you sure, or not sure?'

'I would have to consider the problem. I am not sufficiently expert, sir.'

'But it might be possible?'

'In electronics many things are.'

'Thank you, John. That's a good enough answer for me.'

14

Robin kept his next appointment with Dr Walker on a Monday morning. He was expected at Southwood Hospital at eleven o'clock. He travelled by a nine-thirty train from Boroughfare Tube station. There were some commuters and a lot of shoppers on his train, in other words numbers that were safe – he would not have risked a journey inviting further communication from wherever.

He had a wait of a couple of hours before Dr Walker could see him. He was neither impatient nor particularly apprehensive. His nervous energy seemed to have been spent in renouncing God and writing his renunciation for publication. He was relieved to cede responsibility for his existence to the medical profession. He felt unusually passive even by his standards.

Dr Walker asked after Robin, smiled on being told he was not too bad, and pronounced sentence. In his judgment Robin needed a triple bypass: he put it technically, but that was what it boiled down to. He gave a date, it was another fortnight ahead, and said Robin would have to be in hospital for three days before the op and for at least two weeks afterwards. Was he willing to agree to such a procedure?

Robin said yes.

They shook hands, and Dr Walker handed him over to a nurse for tests and for passing him on to a radiologist. Robin left the hospital at twelve-thirty, and, instead of heading for the Tube, asked for and followed directions to the bus stop where he could catch a bus to Boroughfare. He was determined not to find himself again alone on a train platform in the bowels of the earth.

A bus came along, a double-decker, and he climbed aboard and mounted the stairs to the top deck. He walked to the front seat. Nobody else was up there, but he had enjoyed such front seats of buses ever since childhood, and he was not going to have his enjoyment compromised today by – perhaps literally – the fear of God.

He had stuck to his guns so far. He had not wavered in his commitment to anti-religion. He was brave – or was it bravado? He was tempted to issue one of those challenges issued by blasphemous children of all ages: 'Let God strike me dead for saying He does not exist!'

The bus moved off in a clatter of diesel engine and a cloud of choking fumes. Robin told himself that he was glad to be on that bus, seeing the sights. When he was halfway home, the bus pulled away from a bus stop with a particularly loud revving of its engine, and he was being spoken to.

The voice was familiar, it followed on from the noise of the bus, and had a tender inflection.

The message was: 'Forgive me, as you are forgiven.'

This time, for unknown reasons, more unknown reasons, Robin was not startled. He had thought he was dreading the voice, but he was happy to hear it – he had been yearning for it subconsciously. At first it was the tone of the delivery, so tender and personal, so compassionate, that disarmed him. It seemed to peel away inhibitions, the hard skins formed over a long period, and to revise the recent past. He was aware of a lump in his throat, contrarily his happiness made him sad – it was such an age since he had been happy. His feelings were like seeing the oasis after being lost in the desert. His feelings were boyish – he was reminded of being happy and sad simultaneously when he was a boy. The lump swelled in his throat and a sob escaped him. He glanced round; no passengers had joined him on the top deck. He began to sob uncontrollably, half-laughing at himself as he reached for his handkerchief.

And he registered the message, which reinforced with words the sounds of the voice. It absolved him. It forgave him for writing against God. It freed him from the defeatism of his life. It could not be a trick – was too good for tricks – hit too many nails on the head – was too essential. Only intelligence that could read his mind and be cognisant of his psyche would have known how deeply in need of forgiveness he had been, forgiveness for his sins of omission, for having been so unappreciative of the gift of his existence.

But the message also pleaded for forgiveness.

Robin was asked by his mentor and the author of heaven-sent messages to be forgiven. He was moved again to think that God in His Almightiness, accused of every crime under the sun by the descendants of Adam and Eve, not least by the occupant of The Nest in Roebuck Road, should meekly seek absolution as well as granting it.

He wiped his eyes and stepped off the bus in Boroughfare. He did some shopping in Tesco's and hurried home, luckily without meeting anyone who knew him. He ate lunch, cheese and fruit, and went up to his bedroom to rest. It was not a sign of collapse or even of illness, although his heart hammered when it felt like it and distressed him, but of preparing for a labour of love, gathering the energy he was going to need. At four-thirty he got up and went downstairs, refreshed by sleep, and made himself a mug of tea. He took the mug and some Rich Tea biscuits into his front room, drew the curtains, and settled down at his desk.

Two contracts had arrived from *Beyond*. One was signed by Suejoe and seemed to be in order. She had referred to his article thus: 'Mysterious Voices from the Other World'. He crossed it out in both copies and wrote instead, 'A miracle for me', signed the other copy and sealed it in the envelope provided.

He turned his attention to the writing he had done in the previous week. On a new page of a new pad of the lined paper he used he wrote his new title and began again.

'I am sixty years of age, and live alone in a terrace house in North London. I venture to call myself a religious historian, an historian of religions, but very little of my work has ever been published. I have led a quiet life, my disposition is reclusive, and I have recently received four supernatural communications. And I hereby swear before my God that I am telling and will tell the truth.'

He copied out his accounts of messages one, two and three, and wrote another of message four.

He then embarked on an up-to-date version of his preoccupations.

'Those are the facts to which I bear witness. But my facts – or yours, for that matter – may not be incontrovertible copper-bottomed records of events. Nobody can corroborate my four experiences, nobody was present at crucial moments, the only person who might have been within earshot of message one heard nothing. I therefore have to declare that the rest of this article will be autobiographical, the story of my own reactions, interpretations, sentiments and beliefs. In almost the same breath I wish to assure my readers and hope to convince them that I am not an egoist.

'The four messages reached me in precisely twenty-six days. They succeeded each other after intervals of irregular duration. All the messages shocked me, but each in a different way. I feel certain, but only time will tell, that the fourth message is the last I shall receive.

'I chose to believe that the first was supernatural. I considered other possibilities and the sceptical scenarios put forward by friends and advisers. But I have no history of psychological disturbance or psychic power, and trickery could not be substantiated. Alternatively, nobody understands the social system in force in the next world – a crown prince there might not be quite the same as a crown prince here; and the breeding of Jesus lent credence to the theory that a middle-class sixty-year-old, a hermit by inclination and a failure, could be a sort of princeling in the heavenly hierarchy. At least the vocalist had some knowledge of the New Testament in the King James translation. The words "my kingdom" seemed to come straight out of the Christian Bible, and the Lord's Prayer in particular. I therefore jumped halfway to the conclusion that God had addressed me, and was thrilled, elated, and confused by my unworthiness, as words cannot convey.

'The second message, "Teach the people", had a Biblical ring. I was pleased beyond belief to feel that, in spite of my shortcomings, I had been chosen to pass on the news that God had reminded a godless world of His existence by speaking to me. But I did wonder why an omniscient being had picked on a man of my age, in poor health, not a pedagogue, and shy to the point of shunning other people, to deputise for probably the greatest of all teachers. Dangerous doubt, infectious doubt, mingled with my delight.

'The third message qualifies as a personal

disaster. A seat in Paradise was bad enough, a reserved seat was worse – incredible, laughable.

'A mystery is a lovesome thing, and all religions are mysterious, but the line that divides mysteries from fantasies, fibs and untruths is uncomfortably close.

'Just possibly God in His wisdom was teasing me, and He and His angels were taking a break in order to pull my leg. I began to think I had missed the point, and that I was somehow the butt of a hoax.

'The disastrousness consisted of the effect of these three messages on my faith. I had gone up in the world, and dropped down from a great height. I sank far lower than the lowness of my pre-princely existence. The Christian religion had resembled the skeleton of my intellectual and emotional existence. From the time of my christening, although I never thought of becoming a priest or a monk, I was supported, reinforced, held in an upright position, and kept going by Christianity. Message three smashed everything. The more I thought about it, the more of my life and reasons for living I saw scattered far and wide in the form of bones and ashes.

'It was unbearable. I had been too high to consent to being left to moulder in the pit. I rebelled – and I was asked to write about my "voices" and their consequences. I yielded to temptation with a will. The thirty years of my researches into the history of religions would not be wasted. That huge body of work, hundreds of thousands of instances of mankind's love of

203

God and attempts to please Him and win His favour, testimony to the aspirations of our race to be good and to better themselves, I re-interpreted, turned upside down, and distilled into a more realistic testament.

'I denied God. I wrote for *Beyond* a denial of God. It was terrible to discover that every belief, however strong, can become disbelief by pressing a small mental switch. Synonyms have antonyms, and faith is the twin of faithlessness. How obvious! How mind-stretching for me! I could not stomach the New Testament, the Virgin Birth, the Resurrection. The rites of the Church ceased to be traditional and looked primitive to my incredulous eye. The blood involved in religions, blood drunk, blood-letting, blood shed in the names of Gods, offended me. My messages were somehow the product of the modern mystery of science. I could accept such an explanation as readily as I had accepted that God created the world in seven days. Science seemed preferable, and I proclaimed my atheism.

'I suppose the time that followed could be called a dark night of the soul. I put my article in the envelope provided by *Beyond*, but did not seal or post it. I then kept an appointment with my cardiologist. On the way home, in the bus after I had been told I would be having open-heart surgery in a matter of days, I received message four.

'It was the end of my story and the beginning. The voice had been indescribably, irresistibly sweet. The divinity of it was the plea for my

204

forgiveness, the humility, the attribution of power to me to forgive the Lord God of Hosts. I was absolved of my sins for frittering my life, and for rejecting religion altogether. The "you" who was forgiven, me, I believed, was also plural, everybody, all the sinners killing one another in the names of religion, all the bloody people, and all that I had found fault with in religious institutions.

'My atheism was short-lived. I arrived home and tore up the atheistic part of my article for *Beyond*. Thank God, I had not posted it.

'My "voice" rescued me from the desert of atheism. Atheists think they are cleverer than superstitious godly folk, but having no answers whatsoever is stupider than having some good ones and some that are not good. Too late I remembered my Uncle Willy's funeral in a pseudo-chapel in a crematorium. Uncle Willy was an atheist, the proselytising sort, who assured churchgoers that they were damn fools. His funeral was the drabbest dreariest ceremony, and should have put me off atheism for ever.

'I must confess that I have not done much teaching, disregarding the injunction of message two. I have merely passed through a period of extraordinary vicissitudes, and now conclude my overlong if abridged account of it. And I dare to ask myself if that is the lesson which I was required to teach. Anyone kind enough to have read so far will have to tailor the lesson to fit individual circumstances. Religion is not logical, but is nonetheless part of the most private life of God's creatures, human and perhaps animal. It is a secret garden where weary travellers find a spring of pure cool water with which to refresh themselves.

'Belatedly, I acknowledge that religions have to have leaders. They have to have priests, congregations, money, buildings, organisations and bureaucracy. My religion was inherited, inculcated, habitual. My four messages gave me back the magical element mislaid in my youth. A miracle for me has been the process of rediscovery. God had seemed superfluous to my requirements. But He was my guide to where I am pleased to be at present and, I believe, will be in the future.'

Robin finished his article late on the Thursday evening. He was not well, and he was exhausted. He retired to bed and fell asleep or into a coma. On Friday he was not up to much and confined to quarters, as military-minded Max would have said. But on Saturday he felt better and was able to post his article. Tesco's had its tonic effect, and back in The Nest he rang his cousins to invite them to supper on Sunday evening.

They both complained of the short notice they were given. Zinnia scolded and Max insisted on checking in his diary that he would be available.

Eventually he said: 'Yes, I could manage that. Thank you, Robin. I'm having drinks with the Butler-Hennessys earlier in the evening. They're my friends from the frozen north. What time did you have in mind?'

'As usual,' Robin replied, 'except that I'll be there before you – we'll meet at Ab's Caf.'

'Oh – really? – if you say so – see you then!'

Zinnia accepted the invitation, and asked: 'Is Max coming?'

'Yes.'

'You've invited him, too?'

'That's nothing new.'

'Poor Max, he does try to keep his nose above water.'

'He's trying sometimes, I admit. Who are the Butler-Hennessys?'

'Who?'

'The Butler-Hennessys – his friends from the frozen north.'

'Are they Eskimos?'

'Ask me another! Max is having drinks with them on Sunday evening.'

'Heaven help us if he has one too many.'

They giggled.

'Same time, same place, I suppose?' she inquired.

'Not quite, I'll wait for you at Ab's.'

'Goodness, Robin! No meeting at The Nest – why are you breaking the habit of a lifetime?'

'Wait and see.'

He rang off, they rang off.

Sunday dawned, and he struggled along to the early service at St Columb's. After the twenty-or-so other communicants had exchanged greetings with Hubert Greenstock as he stood by the door of the church, Robin walked slowly down the aisle, leaning on his stick.

'I'm sorry to see you in this state,' Hubert said, referring to his slow progress.

'It's temporary, I hope,' Robin replied. 'I'm having an operation this coming week.'

'Good, good,' Hubert commented dismissively, revealing a healthy interest in the breakfast that Dorothea was no doubt preparing in the vicarage.

They shook hands.

But Hubert turned back and inquired: 'Oh Robin, I forgot – your voices – have you heard them again?'

'Not to speak of,' Robin replied. 'Past history, Hubert – I'm not delving into it any more.'

'Ah yes – you're probably wise. Good morning and good luck!'

Robin did not disagree with Hubert.

At home he ate his own breakfast, and rested in his front room.

The doorbell rang.

He huffed and puffed to his door and asked: 'Who is it?'

'Wendy, Mr Antrobus.'

He opened his door.

'Wendy Paddle was standing outside with John Patterson.

'We are bothering you, sir. We will go away if you are busy.'

'It's all right,' he wheezed. 'Come in.'

He led them into his front room.

'Please sit down,' he said. 'Wendy, you there, John, there, and I'll sit here.'

'Sir,' John said, 'you are not well – we must go away.'

'Don't, please! I have time. My heart is weak, but I'm having an operation in a few days. Did you come for any special reason?'

Robin addressed Wendy, who said as if with bashfulness: 'John will tell you, Mr Antrobus.'

John said: 'Sir, Wendy has agreed to marry me one day.'

'Congratulations!'

'It is in principle, sir. But I cannot change my religion, although I disagree with some of its regulations.'

Robin asked Wendy: 'Are you changing yours?'

'That's the problem.'

'Would you be an atheist?'

'Oh no, sir.'

'What would you change to?'

'Help me, please, sir!'

'The Imam from the Mosque came to see me. He was rather alarming.'

'It is what I do not like, sir.'

'I cannot advise you, Wendy. I'm a private individual, not a counsellor.'

'But you know God, sir, and God knows you.'

'Knowing is difficult. I hope God knows me, and I choose to know Him. Incidentally, John, I've chosen to believe that my voices were not electronic, although I can't know for certain who spoke to me. What can I say to you, Wendy? The other day I thought of denying my religion, but I can't, it's my youth and memories, it's myself. And I'm glad I can't. But that's only my experience.'

'Thank you, sir.'

She smiled at Robin, and they all stood up and shook hands.

Robin asked: 'Would you like to stay with me for a little while?'

John said: 'Another day, sir – we would not tire you. We wish you well for your operation. We are both so grateful.'

15

Robin walked with difficulty to Ab's Caf on the Sunday evening. He stopped several times to take deeper breaths: He had decided to walk to the restaurant alone – he would tell his cousins about his health and everything else when he was sitting down, not as he wheezed and coughed in the roadway.

The restaurant was open but empty. Debra stood listlessly behind the coffee-making machine on the bar. Miriam was berating Ab in the kitchen. Debra smirked at Robin. The relative silence was broken only by the clang of cooking utensils and muzak. Ab emerged, tying on his white neck-to-ankles apron and throwing up his hands to indicate pleasure at the sight of a customer. He expressed a hope that Mr Robin was going to be joined by Mr Max and Miss Zinnia. He looked more henpecked than ever. His wisps of hair did not lie flat on his scalp and his lower lip hung loose.

Coincidentally he showed concern for Robin just as Robin was feeling concerned for him.

'My God, may I say how bad you look? What have they done to you? Have a drink, sir – my treat!'

Robin declined and explained.

'Heart surgery is not a joke,' Ab commented in his encouraging vein. 'You better have a good big meal tonight.'

'Not too big,' Robin said.

An idea occurred to Ab – he struck his forehead with the fist of his hand.

'I'll pay you back for not being rude about my religion, Mr Robin, when you spoke in your sister's flat. You gave a lovely speech, and I'll give you a lovely little dinner tonight. You're friendly with God, so God will be friendly to me for feeding you. It's a bargain. Is Mr Max coming along?'

'He is, and Zinnia too – thank you for the offer, Ab – but you can't give all three of us dinner.'

'True, sir. I'll speak with Miriam. She's my bank manager' – he lowered his voice and looked nervously over his shoulder – 'only worse.'

He laughed and returned to the kitchen. Robin's cousins did not arrive – Zinnia was not punctual. Debra inquired from behind the bar 'if he wanted bread at all?' Ab reappeared with Miriam in tow – he so wasted and pale, she so stout and ruddy.

Miriam exclaimed or, rather, lamented: 'Oh you poor man – surgery! What's your God got to say about that? What are we going to do without you on Sunday evenings?'

Ab addressed her: 'Could we help Mr Robin with the bill?'

Robin said: 'You don't need to, honestly!'

Miriam addressed Ab: 'He doesn't need that

sort of help – see? I've some chicken soup, Mr Robin, you're welcome to the soup.'

Ab warned her: 'We're serving three – his cousins are on the way.'

'Three, is it?' she said. 'I'll do free soup for two.'

Ab spoke to Robin as Miriam retired to the kitchen and the restaurant door opened: 'Better than nothing, I hope you'll agree, sir.'

'Thank you, Ab,' Robin replied.

He then had to withstand assaults on his looks and health from his cousins.

Robin checked them by saying: 'Ab and Miriam have been burying me, so don't you start!'

The others removed outer garments, entrusted them to Ab and Debra, joined Robin at their usual table and sat down.

The news of the operation was broken.

'Why didn't you tell us?' Zinnia grumbled. 'You might have let us know that you were that ill. I thought you were recuperating after your heart attack, and getting on fine. Suddenly you're looking rotten and in for a major op.'

Max took a different line in order to discomfort Robin.

'I suppose you've had a second opinion? Always best to have a second opinion when the quacks are trying to get their knives into you!'

Robin replied first to Zinnia.

'What would you have done if I'd told you how ill I was?'

'I could have come round and seen you, I could have cosseted you.'

213

'Oh, Zinnia, I haven't been strong enough to be cosseted by your kind self.'

They all laughed.

He turned to Max and said: 'Lucky for everyone that you're only a company doctor!'

They laughed again.

'Tell us now,' Zinnia suggested.

He gave them a digest of his tests, Dr Walker's less optimistic diagnoses, and the pains and breathlessness that were quite likely to be cured by the bypass operation scheduled for the end of the coming week.

Max said: 'Next week? Isn't that rushing it? If you can't get a second opinion, you could have second thoughts.'

Zinnia asked: 'Do you know what day you go into Southwood hospital?'

'It could be Wednesday.'

'So is this the last time we see you – I mean, before the operation?'

Robin laughed, and Ab approached with pen and pencil poised.

Zinnia and Max both wanted escalope of veal. Their orders were redolent of auld lang syne, as if they were about to eat food at a wake. Robin branched out, and caused the cousins' eyebrows to be raised suspiciously, by ordering ham, eggs, baked beans and chips. The cousins were not soup drinkers, but jumped at such a first course when Robin revealed that it was partly a presentation from the management.

Max commented when Ab was out of earshot: 'Never overlook a gift horse in the mouth.'

'Look, not overlook,' Zinnia corrected him. 'And your dinner's solid cholesterol, Robin.'

'Why not? I'm undergoing surgery for high cholesterol. Besides, as you pointed out, this may be our last supper.'

'I corrected myself – before the op, I said.'

'Yes – well – you were always pedantic, Zinnia.'

'I'm not heartless.'

'But I could well be,' he responded, and their laughter turned into the family giggle.

Zinnia offered Robin belated sympathy, and Max mumbled that he knew too well how hellish it was to feel seedy.

Then Zinnia inquired: 'What's God got to say about your health?'

Max chimed in: 'My experience is that you can't see God for dust when you're ill.'

Robin hesitated before saying, 'Somebody spoke to me again.'

'Who spoke to you?' Max inquired, and Zinnia snapped at him, 'Who do you think, Dumbo!'

'I heard the voice,' Robin revealed, 'in a bus on the way back from Southwood Hospital.'

'Giving you another message?' Zinnia asked.

'Yes.'

'What was it?'

' "Forgive me, as you're forgiven".'

'How peculiar!'

'I believe it's the final message.'

'Why?'

'I don't know why. There's no "why" in all that's happened to me. It's a secret. Life's a mystery. Platitudes and truisms are the only explanation of everything that's deep and interesting. Feelings, emotions, guesses, intuition, they're religion, they are, in a nutshell. I feel I won't hear the voice any more.'

'Golly!' Max said. 'The gospel according to Robin,' he added, but Zinnia frowned at him and said: 'What does it mean? What did it mean to you?'

'I've written an article that tries to explain its meaning.'

'Where?'

'In a magazine called *Beyond*.'

Max said: 'It's beyond me, that's for sure.'

Zinnia asked Robin: 'Do you think it was God asking to be forgiven?'

'I believe so.'

'For speaking to you? For saying ridiculous things to you?'

'Maybe for more than that. Maybe because of the tragedies and the tears.'

'Goodness me!' Zinnia exclaimed.

'Look here,' Max put in, 'what's God forgiving you for, Robin? You've lived your whole life in The Nest, you've never left The Nest, if you'll pardon me for saying so, and you've always gone to your church. If it wasn't God forgiving you, I'd say it was cheek.'

'Oh Max,' Zinnia sighed.

Robin said: 'I was an atheist.'

At this point Ab arrived with the wine, then Debra served the soup – small helpings, soon drunk – and the food followed without delay. The two Joneses downed wine as if it were

216

medicine, a prescription for the alleviation of shock, and tackled their victuals as if to gain strength. The conversation was desultory during a type of interval. Max seized his chance to say how ill he was. Zinnia called him a hypochondriac, and they had half a tiff between mouthfuls. When the main course was eaten, two ices and a Peach Melba were ordered and consumed.

Zinnia spoke.

'Robin, you were saying? What were you saying? I thought for a mad moment you said you were an atheist.'

'It's true,' he replied. 'At least it was true. And I must have committed other sins, and I was so pleased to be forgiven. But my understanding is that the forgiveness extended farther afield, that God begged us to forgive Him for all the suffering and that he was forgiving us for often being so awful.'

'If that was what you understood – such wonderful things about God – why did you reject Him?'

'I yielded to the temptation to blame Him. I blamed Him instead of blaming myself. I blamed Him for everything ever since He created Eve so silly that she was conned by the snake.'

'Did you write stuff like that in your article?'

'Yes. No. I wrote it and tore it up. The final article tries to explain why I did both. Once you start blaming God, it's difficult to stop. But I did stop, and that's the point. *Beyond* ought to have my work by now, and I've had no complaints. We should get a copy one day.'

'This *Beyond*, Robin, is it reputable? Are they paying you?'

'Good old Max! You're right to bring us down to earth. It's where I want to be for as long as possible. Yes, they're paying. They're paying seven thousand five hundred pounds.'

'They're not!'

'I'm giving it to you.'

'What? Sorry, what was that?'

'I haven't received the money yet, but I have a contract, and here it is.' He produced it from his pocket. 'Zinnia, you hang on to it. Contact *Beyond* if payment's delayed. The money should come to The Nest, but more than likely after I'm in hospital. I'm going to give you power of attorney to look after things for me, pay bills and sign cheques, in my absence. I trust you, but Lindsey Addiscombe will be keeping an eye on my bank account and ensuring there's money available. The seven and a half thousand pounds is to clear Max's debts, and the rest is for you and Max to share and use as you wish.'

'Bless my soul!' Max said, and Zinnia: 'I'm sure you can't afford to give so much money away, Robin.'

'True,' he answered her, laughing. 'I was tempted to keep it, but I couldn't make a habit of yielding to temptation, and I can't make money out of God.'

She turned to her brother and asked: 'Can we accept such a big present?'

Max cleared his throat and replied: 'Robin's being damn generous, and he's worked it all out.

218

Personally, I'm not going to cross him, so thanks be, and God knows I need the money.'

Zinnia turned to Robin.

'Is it really okay?'

'Yes.'

'Thank you.'

Robin coughed. Zinnia said it was high time for him to be at home and in bed. They stood up, Robin paid the bill at the bar, Debra brought coats, and Ab fetched Miriam from the kitchen. At the door Zinnia and Max were bowed out, Debra helped Robin into his British Warm and handed him his pork-pie and his stick, and Miriam embraced him tightly and said: 'Mr Robin, you come back to us, please – it'll be a free dinner then, remember.' Ab shook his hand between both of his, and waved good-night from the doorway.

The cousins headed homewards.

Zinnia folded Robin's free arm in hers and said: 'I hate to see the stick.'

'Sorry,' he returned.

'Am I walking too fast?'

'No.'

Max remarked: 'They tell me your op's not too nasty, and they have you on your feet the day after.'

'Thank you, Max.'

'No, old boy, no – other way round – and always has been. Don't you worry! I'll be having your op in a year or two, I shouldn't wonder.'

The pavement narrowed in Roebuck Road, and Max fell behind the other two.

Zinnia squeezed Robin's arm and asked: 'Are you a special person after all?'

He laughed – he was laughing particularly at the last two words, 'after all'.

'Am I going to have to be proud of you?' she persisted.

'No,' he laughed again and continued. 'I'm a nine days wonder. *Beyond*'s an international magazine, based in the United States, and must have a tiny circulation here – I'd never heard of it before it contacted me. I'll never tell my story again, so I won't become public property if I survive.'

'I wish you wouldn't talk of survival.'

'Why not? It doesn't matter, one way or the other. What about yourself, now and in future?'

'Oh I'm fine. Actually I've met a man I like, another man – but hope springs eternal. And I've got Max to look after.'

They reached The Nest.

'Good-night,' she said; 'no goodbyes – good-night, darling,' and kissed him with unusual warmth.

Max shook his hand and said: 'You sleep tight – I don't think your dinner was indigestible.'

Robin went in and locked his front door.

The next day, Monday, he received notification from Southwood Hospital that he had to check in on Thursday midday, bringing a minimum of luggage, and that the operation was booked for next Saturday or the following Monday. It recommended no visitors before the operation, since he would be kept busy with tests.

He telephoned Lindsey Addiscombe and arranged everything. Lindsey promised to put the form relating to power of attorney in the post immediately. He wished Robin the best of luck.

Robin did not leave home on that day. He was too tired, and felt more impatient than anything else, impatient to set off on his journey to God knew where.

On Tuesday he felt stronger. He rang the Padger sisters, who hoped that he would soon be back in The Nest – strange hopes considering that they never met and seldom set eyes on one another.

In the evening he rang the Rickitts. Bill's reaction was to bawl, 'Happy landings!' above the noise of pop music and family argument.

Robin also wrote a note to Dylan Murphy, suggesting a postponement of lunch at the Priest's House. He did not decline it, he felt he now had nothing to fear from that quarter, since he intended to make no further comment on supernatural matters and tread on no more religious toes.

On the Wednesday he walked to Boroughfare and asked Jayendra Patel for his bill, that is the money he owed for a variety of his purchases over the last months.

Jayendra said: 'I'm so happy to see you, Mr Antrobus – and not because of the money, sir. I would have telephoned if you had not come in. Mr Ab at the restaurant has told me you are to be in hospital.'

Robin explained why.

'Oh Mr Antrobus, sir, get well soon.'

Robin began to write his cheque.

'How's Wendy?' he asked.

'We cannot get used to that name, sir – but she is in good health. Mr Antrobus, I think we are in debt to you. Indira may marry Jehan in our Mosque. It was our wish, but we are English and would not arrange her marriage. They say you have helped to solve the problem of religion.'

'I've only let them talk to me, Jayendra.'

'Indira will not change all things at once. She is going to be a solicitor, not a beautician. She says you have helped her to decide.'

'I'm glad. She's a clever girl as well as a nice one. Please convey my congratulations.'

'Yes, Mr Antrobus. Sir, how long will you be away from your home?'

'Oh, I don't know, some weeks or longer, until I can manage on my own.'

'I will ask something, Mr Antrobus, on condition you promise to answer me yes or no. I would not offend you, or be offended.'

'Ask away! Here's my cheque.'

'Thank you, sir. Indira has to earn money to pay for her legal study. She will work with us in the shop – it will be convenient, you see. But it would be more convenient if she lived closer, but not at home. Would you allow her to live in your house when you are absent?'

'It's an idea.'

'Have you a spare room, sir?'

'Yes, upstairs, two bedrooms, but they have not been used for a long time.'

'Indira would clean them, she would clean your house – she is very clean – and pay market rent.'

'Jayendra, I go into hospital tomorrow, and have no time to do business.'

'Sir, Sanjana and I could bring Indira to see you this evening. The business could be done in ten minutes, if you were agreeable. If you do not agree, we would leave with no hard feelings. I promise we would not stay long. I hope you will not be worried. The arrangement would be good for all, Mr Antrobus.'

'Come at six-thirty.'

'Thank you, sir. Indira will be joyful to see you. But we will expect neither yes nor no. How do you go to hospital tomorrow? Is it Southwood Hospital?'

'I'll book a taxi to take me to Southwood.'

'I could drive you, sir.'

'Thanks, Jayendra, but I think I'll be braver alone. See you later!'

He walked back to Roebuck Road. It was eleven in the morning, and the sun pierced through the clouds and still shed a little warmth. He wondered if he should say a prayer in St Columb's; but Hubert Greenstock might be there, and he walked slowly with the aid of his stick past The Nest, rounded Roebuck Buildings, hoping not to see or be seen by Max, and in the Rec returned to the seat on which he had been told he was not a failed scribbler of three score years but a crown prince.

He heard sounds that affected him unexpectedly.

A shop somewhere was blasting out a rendering of Jingle Bells; but distance enhanced it. The faint sounds reminded him that Christmas was not far off. Christmas was another reminder, a two-fold reminder, the first religious, the second that at Christmastime there was always one day hinting prematurely at spring. He was moved to wonder whether or not he would join in the celebrations of either the birth of the more legitimate Son of God, or the season of new life.

Anyway, he looked forward to the future.

The sun warmed the cockles of the organ that did not know what it was in for. Robin felt his responsibilities recede. They, and his cares and mistakes, seemed to bow out of his presence. He tried to remember that other person who had sat where he was sitting long ago, in another age, during a thunderstorm. He wondered idly, and was moved to realise he was enjoying himself thoughtlessly, as he had not done perhaps ever.

He had no need to hurry anywhere. He had time to book his taxi. He blinked in the sunshine and smiled at passers-by. Eventually he remembered food for his supper, and hobbled along to Tesco's.

29. 3. 06